JUL 3 0 1999

D1637301

A HANDFUL OF TROUBLE

*Also by Cathie Linz
in Large Print:*

Continental Lover
One of a Kind Marriage
Pride and Joy
Tender Guardian
Wildfire

This Large Print Book carries the
Seal of Approval of N.A.V.H.

A HANDFUL OF TROUBLE

Cathie Linz

Thorndike Press • Thorndike, Maine

Published in 1999 by arrangement with Cathie Linz.

Thorndike Large Print ® Americana Series.

The tree indicium is a trademark of Thorndike Press.

The text of this Large Print edition is unabridged.
Other aspects of the book may vary from the original edition.

Set in 16 pt. Plantin by Rick Gundberg.

Printed in the United States on permanent paper.

Library of Congress Cataloging in Publication Data

Linz, Cathie.
  A handful of trouble / Cathie Linz.
    p. cm.
  ISBN 0-7862-2021-X (lg. print : hc : alk. paper)
  1. Large type books. I. Title.
  [PS3562.I558H36 1999]
  813´.54—dc21   99-27635

A HANDFUL
OF TROUBLE

CHAPTER ONE

Josh Phillips was jogging along the only road curving Bermuda's southern shore when he suddenly saw a blurred figure out of the corner of his eye. Some idiot on a moped was headed straight for him!

There wasn't time to think, only to act. Using a move that had helped him score a winning touchdown at UCLA over a decade ago, Josh made a flying leap to the roadside.

He barely made it in time. The moped came so close to him that Josh felt the hot whoosh of air from its exhaust pipe before he hit the ground. A second later he heard the sound of skidding tires and the wrench of abused metal. Then all was quiet as the moped's engine abruptly cut out.

Spitting the dust from his mouth, Josh cautiously got to his feet. Prior experience on the football field, and now on the often volatile oil fields where he worked, had taught him how to take a fall. The same couldn't be said for the driver of the kamikaze moped, who lay sprawled facedown a short distance from the mishandled vehicle. What had the idiot been thinking of, veering off the road like that?

Curbing his anger for the moment, Josh knew his first priority was to make sure that the driver hadn't suffered any serious injuries. He couldn't tell much from this vantage point. All he could see was a motorcycle helmet and the back of a T-shirt. As Josh drew closer, he automatically checked the driver's legs, searching for the awkward angles that denoted broken limbs. Beneath their denim covering, the long legs appeared to be in alignment. They also appeared to belong to a woman — a shapely woman.

A moment later Josh's supposition was confirmed by the sound of an unmistakably feminine voice muttering some very unfeminine curses as she sat up and fumbled to undo the strap of her helmet.

"Are you hurt?" Josh's question contained the slightest edge of laughter beneath the concern. Whoever this woman was, she swore like a trooper.

Pam Warner heard the laughter and resented it. "I'm fine. Just dandy!" Finally releasing the stubborn strap, Pam impatiently tugged the helmet from her head. Her curly brown hair fell into eyes that were a shade or two darker.

This had not been her day. She'd been in Bermuda only a few hours and already she'd hit a major snag in her investigation. At least she hadn't hit anything else, no thanks to the jogger who'd been obliviously trotting along the roadside. She'd yelled out a warning to him, but he'd either ignored her or hadn't heard her. Still, she had been able to miss him. And although it felt like she'd bruised every bone in her body, it didn't feel like she'd broken anything. Thank heaven for small favors.

Immediately Pam's thoughts jumped ahead to her next course of action. Providing that the moped was still road worthy, she'd ride it back to her hotel. It wasn't that far away. If the moped was out of commission, she'd flag down a taxi or a bus. Though there weren't any cars on the road just now, she was sure it wouldn't be long before someone came by. Accustomed to taking care of herself, the idea of asking the jogger for help didn't even occur to her.

A lot of ideas were occurring to that jogger as he took a moment to appreciate the woman sitting before him. While she was not classically beautiful, she radiated a passion for life that he found very sexy. Her dark hair was wild and free, adding to her untamed image. His eyes made a slow exploration of her face, noting her dark eyes and full mouth before his gaze wandered over her body. Now that she was facing him, he was able to savor the sight of her very feminine form beneath the T-shirt and dusty jeans. Sultry. Very sultry.

Pam, unaware that she was the center of his attention, was about to get up when the jogger clamped an authoritative hand over her leg.

"You'd better sit still while I check and make sure you haven't broken anything," he told her. "That was quite a fall you took, you know."

"I know." Pam glared at his hand and then at him. She hated being restrained by anybody, and the condescending inflection in this man's voice only added insult to injury. What did he think she was, a half-wit?

Her resentment was clear to Josh, and it was as irresistible to him as a red flag was to a bull. He deliberately took his time completing his examination, moving his fingers over her long legs with roguish thoroughness. When his provocative touch neared the forbidden territory of her inner thigh, Pam grabbed his hand and pushed it aside.

"Listen, buddy, you can go play touchy-feely with somebody else!" she growled. "I'm not in the mood, got that?"

Josh found himself grinning at her blunt rejection. She certainly didn't mince her words. He liked that. He also liked the sexy feel of her body beneath his hands. "Take it easy. My name's Josh, not Buddy, and you may not

10

have broken anything, but you've got a couple of nasty bruises."

"Not where you were looking for them, I don't!"

"Listen, lady," Josh returned in a mocking imitation of her earlier comment, "you're the one who tried to run me over, not vice versa."

"I was not trying to run you over," Pam retorted. To herself she admitted that now that she'd met him, the idea did have some appeal. She'd dealt with this guy's type before. Macho was their middle name and hunting women was their game. Experience had taught them to be cocky, and their approach was always smooth and confident.

Of course, guys like him were good-looking — it was a requirement, one he certainly fulfilled. Sun-bleached hair, blue eyes and brawny muscles — he had them all. He also had a bad-boy gleam in those blue eyes that was accompanied by a wicked grin. All this wrapped up in a six-foot muscle-bound package that was designed to make any woman's heart pound.

Sure, she knew the type, all right. In charge. In control. "In the way," she muttered, glaring at his handsome face.

"What?"

"You were in the way," Pam repeated. "If you had been jogging down at the beach

11

where you belong, instead of along the road, I wouldn't have crashed."

"I hate to differ with you, but the way you were driving you would have crashed regardless. You really should stay off that bike until you're more familiar with driving on the left-hand side of the road."

"My driving is fine!" Pam declared angrily.

Josh eyed the dented moped with a mocking shake of his head. "I don't think the moped rental place is going to agree with you."

Pam was not about to let his comment go unchallenged. "The accident was not my fault! I was trying to avoid getting hit by those two mopeds that were passing an oncoming bus. Surely you saw them?"

"All I saw was you, coming right at me."

Outrage masked the aches and pains that she was beginning to feel all over her body. "You don't believe me!"

"Calm down; I didn't say that." Josh ran a soothing hand over her bare arm. "It doesn't take much to get you riled up, does it?"

"A little thing like an accident is generally sufficient to 'rile me up,' as you put it," Pam declared tartly. "I'm funny that way."

"You're funny in a lot of ways," he noted in a soft voice. "But this isn't really the time to go into that." Josh's hand shifted along her arm, bending it with gentle care. "In case you

12

hadn't noticed, your elbow received a pretty bad scrape and it's bleeding. I think we'd better get you to a doctor."

"I don't need to go to a doctor."

Josh ignored her protests and calmly flagged down a cruising taxi. The move didn't surprise Pam. Taxis always appeared out of nowhere for guys like this.

"Do you think you can get up by yourself?" he asked her. "Or will you need help?" Having made the polite inquiry, he then disregarded her assertion that she could make it by herself and scooped her up in his arms and carried her toward the waiting taxi.

"Why did you even bother asking if you already knew what you were going to do?" she demanded, infuriated by his high-handed behavior.

He turned his head and grinned. "I was giving you the option of coming to your senses and being reasonable."

In that exact instant Pam knew she was in trouble. Awareness flooded through her, making her extremely conscious of everything about this man, from his sexy running shorts to the feel of his rippling muscles beneath her fingertips. Suddenly she saw him for the very attractive man he was, and she felt herself weakening. *It's post-trauma shock*, she firmly told herself. *Don't let this guy's sex appeal blind*

*you to reality. He may be a hunk, but domi-
neering men are not your type.*

The silent pep talk didn't work. Her heart was still pounding as Josh carefully lowered her to the seat of the taxi. He deliberately took his time sliding his arms from around her waist, which didn't help her blood pressure any.

"Stay there," he told her, "while I get the driver to help me put your battered moped in the trunk."

"Yes, master," she muttered.

He leaned back down to remind her, "The name's Josh. Josh Phillips." He paused and grinned wickedly. "But you can call me master. And your name is?"

"Pam Warner." Her voice was so cold it burned. "But you can call me Ms. Warner."

His blue eyes crinkled with amusement. "I could, Pam, but I won't."

There you have it in a nutshell, Pam told herself as Josh left to help the taxi driver stash her moped in the trunk. *Josh Phillips could play by the rules, but he won't. So keep up your guard and remember why you're here in Bermuda. Forget everything else.* Good advice, but difficult to follow.

As soon as Josh joined her in the back of the taxi, he made a point of decreasing the distance between them.

"You really didn't have to bundle me into a

14

taxi like this. I'm perfectly capable of finding a doctor's office on my own," Pam informed him with cool disapproval.

"Nonsense. It's the least I can do for the only lady who's ever knocked me off my feet." With seeming nonchalance Josh stretched his arm out across the back of the seat, revealing a tempting view of a muscular torso beneath his tank top. "Besides, if I don't go with you, I have a sneaking suspicion you won't go to a doctor's office at all."

Pam had her own sneaking suspicions to contend with. She knew Josh was deliberately trying to make her aware of him. She also knew that his plan was working, and she didn't like that one bit.

Misinterpreting her frown, Josh asked, "Are you in pain?"

"You could say that," she muttered, angry with herself as much as she was with him. What had happened to her immunity?

"Here." Josh's hand lowered to her shoulder with the intention of easing her closer. "Lean against me."

Pam refused to budge. "Thanks, but no thanks."

Josh shifted so that he was facing her. "What's wrong? You're not afraid of me, are you?"

"Afraid, no. Distrustful, yes. Extremely,"

she stated emphatically.

"Of me?" he asked with exaggerated disbelief. "How come?"

Pam didn't look away from his teasing eyes. Instead she narrowed her own gaze and tried to outstare him. "It might have something to do with the fact that you strong-armed me into this cab. Then again it could have originated with your attempts to play doctor along the roadside."

"I was just trying to be a good Samaritan." Josh's eyes had lowered for a leisurely perusal of her body as he voiced his claim.

"Believe me, I know exactly what you were trying to do," Pam returned. "And being good had nothing to do with it!"

"I'm very good," Josh murmured in a sexy drawl.

"Modest, too," Pam noted with a mocking nod.

Josh's laughter caught her unawares. She hadn't anticipated that it would have such a rich, deep sound or that it would remind her of a cougar's deep-throated purr. *Watch it,* Pam silently ordered herself. *You're treading on dangerous ground here.*

Deciding that silence was the best defense in this case, Pam focused her attention on the passing scenery and wished Josh would do the same. But of course he didn't. He continued to study her boldly, making her acutely aware of her rapid breathing and the rise and fall of her breasts. In the hope of regaining some control over the situation, Pam turned her back on Josh Phillips and continued to stare out the window.

Bermuda in June was lovely. As a travel agent, Pam had booked many vacations to the island, but this was the first time she'd ever been here. Unfortunately her trip wasn't for pleasure; she was in Bermuda on business. And if she didn't succeed in her quest, she'd be out of business! That constant gnawing fear made it difficult to appreciate the beauty of the island.

Judging by the increasing traffic, Pam guessed that their destination was the capital city of Hamilton.

"I really don't have time for this." The words were directed to herself and overheard by Josh.

"It won't take long," he reassured her. "The doctor will have you patched up in no time."

"You don't understand." Pam's expression was one of harried exasperation. "Time is of the essence. I came to Bermuda looking for someone, and I have to find him."

"Him?" Josh repeated suspiciously. "Him who?"

"Roger Bass."

Josh shrugged. "Never heard of him. Why are you looking for him?"

"For personal reasons."

Josh wasn't put off by her curt reply. "How personal?"

"That's really none of your business."

"Sure it is." Once again her disapproval rolled off him like water off a duck. "I need to know if you're married, engaged or involved."

"You may need to know, but I don't need to tell you."

"Ah." He sounded very satisfied.

"Ah, what? What's that supposed to mean?"

"You're not married or engaged; you don't wear a ring." He picked up her hand and displayed her bare ring finger. "And you're not involved or you would have said so."

Pam snatched her hand away from him. "I don't know why I even bother answering your questions," she muttered. "You've already created your own answers."

"I can be quite creative," he murmured in a sexy undertone.

By contrast Pam's voice sounded much louder as she said, "Fine. Go be creative on your own side of the taxi!"

Josh's eyes met those of the sympathetic taxi driver in the rearview mirror. "She's crazy about me."

The driver grinned and nodded.

"If anyone's crazy around here, it's you," Pam informed Josh indignantly.

"Here we are," the taxi driver announced with a flourish as he came to a halt in front of a white one-story building.

"Wait for us," Josh told the driver.

"There's no need for him to wait," Pam protested. She was on a limited budget and didn't want the meter ticking while she was being patched up.

"Oh, I don't mind, ma'am," the driver said with the gentle English accent of a native Bermudian. "I've grown rather intrigued by you two."

"But —"

"Come on, stop stalling," Josh ordered. Taking matters into his own hands, he held her firmly by the arm and marched her into the clinic.

Once inside, Pam's protests were drowned out by the sound of a booming voice. "Josh? Josh Phillips? Good to see you." A doctor with gray hair and a white beard pumped Josh's hand in an enthusiastic greeting. "What have you done to yourself this time?"

"This time it's not me, Doc. It's my companion here. Pam, this is Dr. MacPhearson. Everyone calls him Doc."

"How do you two know each other?" Pam

19

asked Josh with a suspicious look first at him and then at the doctor.

"I've had a few run-ins on a moped myself," Josh admitted.

"That's true," the doctor confirmed. "You Americans often have a hard time conforming to our habit of driving on the left."

Personally, Pam thought Josh had a hard time conforming, period.

"But enough of this chitchat," Doc said. "Come into my examining room and we'll take a look at you."

Pam didn't like the sound of that *we*.

Sure enough, Josh accompanied her right into the examining room. "I don't need an armed escort," Pam told him.

"I'm not armed," Josh replied.

"I don't need an escort at all."

"I need some information for our records," Doc told Pam as he placed a form on a clipboard. "We'll begin with your surname."

"Warner," Josh and Pam said in unison.

When she glared at him, he grinned.

"Your age?" Doc asked.

"Look, do we have to have an audience for this?" Pam demanded of the doctor.

"An audience?" Doc repeated, obviously at a loss.

"I'd like Mr. Phillips to wait outside," Pam stated. *The farther away the better!*

20

"She's shy," Josh explained.

Pam's dark eyes reflected the frustration and indignation she was feeling. "I should warn you, Josh, that I am not shy and I don't get mad — I get even."

"I'm looking forward to it," Josh returned in a low voice.

"Look forward to it outside," she told him.

"Don't you want me to hold your hand when you get your shot?" Josh asked with assumed innocence.

Pam's face paled. "What shot?"

"Tetanus. Unless you've had one recently?"

Pam shook her head. She hated needles. Suddenly holding Josh's hand didn't seem like such a bad idea after all.

"You may stay," she told him.

"I'm glad that's been decided," Doc said. "Maybe I'll record the data later and take a look at your arm first."

"That's okay," Pam replied, eager to postpone the examination and the shot for as long as possible. "Go ahead and fill out the form first."

"Your age?"

"Twenty-five."

"Any allergies?"

"None that I know of." *Except to domineering men like Josh Phillips.*

The doctor asked a few more routine questions, the answers to which were duly noted on his form and in Josh's mind.

"Okay, let's take a look at your arm," Doc said.

Josh's prediction proved to be true; she did need a tetanus shot. She wasn't quite sure how she ended up holding Josh's hand, but hold it she did. Actually she was clutching it with such a death grip that her knuckles were white. Josh didn't complain at the way his fingers were being crushed. Instead he sought to distract her by running his thumb over the back of her hand.

"Don't worry," Josh murmured. "You won't feel a thing."

Pam closed her eyes as the doctor readied the syringe. Her eyes flew open again at the feel of a warm tongue darting between her fingers. Josh had lifted her hand to his lips. Now that he'd gotten her attention, he proceeded to nibble on her index finger. There was something unexpectedly erotic about his teasing assault.

"What do you think you're doing?" she demanded in an unsteady whisper.

"Distracting you," Josh replied, his lips moving against her skin. His blue eyes held hers in a silent form of seduction. She didn't look away; she couldn't. She was momentarily spellbound.

"That wasn't so bad, was it?" Doc asked her.

With some difficulty Pam pulled her gaze from Josh's. "What wasn't so bad?"

"The tetanus shot," Josh answered on Doc's behalf. "I told you that you wouldn't feel anything."

Not feel anything? Pam thought to herself with dismay. She felt too much, more than it was wise to feel with a man like Josh Phillips!

The taxi driver was waiting for Pam and Josh when they left the medical clinic. The sight of the small fortune displayed on the meter did not improve Pam's mood any. In addition to that, her arm was beginning to ache from the tetanus shot and her elbow hurt more now than it had before, thanks to the doctor's thorough cleaning of the scrape.

"You're awfully quiet," Josh commented after helping her into the back of the taxi. "Something wrong?"

"Wrong?" Pam repeated with mocking disbelief. "What makes you think something's wrong? Just because I've flown to Bermuda, crashed a rented moped, been accosted by a bossy jogger and had a tetanus shot, all in the course of one day, that doesn't mean anything's wrong. I'm having a wonderful time. Just wonderful!"

23

"You'll feel better once you've had some rest," Josh murmured in a soothing voice.

"Where to now?" their driver asked Josh.

Josh turned to Pam. "Where are you staying?"

Pam named the large South Shore resort that had offered her a travel agent's discount.

Josh leaned forward to repeat the name for the driver and then sat back, making himself comfortable by stretching out his legs and propping his elbow on the door's armrest. He let his gaze roam over Pam with masculine speculation. "I'm staying there, too."

"Figures," Pam muttered.

"Speaking of figures, yours is something else." His blue eyes held an unmistakably naughty gleam as he made no effort to disguise his frank appraisal. He reached out to tap a teasing finger on her knee. "It's a good thing you were wearing these sturdy jeans or you could really have cut yourself up." His hand shifted to her bare uninjured arm as he softly added, "I'd hate to have anything happen to this smooth skin of yours."

Pam jerked away from his provocative touch and grimaced with pain from her sudden movement. The thought of soaking in a hot tub had never been so appealing. But she knew her chances for a speedy return to the hotel were slim, considering Bermuda's twenty-mile-an-hour speed limit. It was going to be a slow trip!

Josh, meanwhile, did not seem to mind the ride at all, and was continuing his modus operandi to distract and disarm. There was no doubt he was good at it. If it was true that practice made perfect, then obviously Josh Phillips had had lots of practice. But Pam wasn't about to let him practice on her. Giving this guy an inch would be the equivalent of giving him a mile. Look how he'd hustled her into the doctor's office despite her firm statement that she didn't want to go. Clearly Josh was a man used to having his own way. But his way wasn't her way.

"You two known each other long?" The taxi driver, who'd introduced himself as Trevor, broke the deadlock of silence in the backseat.

"No. We don't know each other at all," Pam answered.

"Not yet. But we will," Josh amended.

"No, we won't," Pam denied.

"Maybe the beauty of Bermuda will bring you two closer together. You know, all the moonlit nights, walking along the beach . . ." Trevor's voice trailed off suggestively.

"Bermuda has already brought us as close as we're going to get," Pam retorted.

Trevor shook his head and exchanged a

25

masculine look with Josh that seemed to say, *You've got your work cut out for you.*

"Are you here in Bermuda on vacation?" Trevor asked.

Josh's yes coincided with Pam's no.

Trevor tugged on one ear and murmured, "I see." Casting a look in his rearview mirror, he could practically see the sparks flying between his two passengers.

Once they reached the resort, Josh again overrode Pam's objections and insisted on paying the entire taxi fare himself. He then directed a hotel employee to return the battered moped to the rental agent located on site.

Josh cut off Pam's protests at the pass. "Don't waste your energy arguing with me now. Save it for later, when we're having dinner."

His ploy worked. She temporarily exchanged her anger for incredulity. "What dinner? I never said I'd have dinner with you."

To which he countered, "You never said you wouldn't have dinner with me."

"Well, I'm saying it now. I won't have dinner with you." Having spoken her refusal clearly and emphatically, Pam thought that was an end to the matter.

But Josh was not about to give up that easily. "Why not?"

"Because I don't want to."

"Still distrustful, Pam? Or are you just too scared to explore the attraction between us?"

His softly spoken taunt backfired. Unintentionally Josh had just hit the right button to set her off. "Sure, use that old routine, hoping I'll go out with you just to prove I'm not scared! I hate to break it to you, but that isn't going to work with me," Pam declared. "I don't have to prove anything, to you or anyone else."

"It sounds like I hit a nerve," Josh murmured. "I wonder what it was that you once felt you had to prove."

His perception surprised Pam. She wouldn't have thought that he'd pick up on the underlying emotion in her voice. It made no difference to her decision, however. "You'll just have to keep on wondering," she stated. "I'm going to my room. Good-bye, Josh. I hope you enjoy your stay here in Bermuda."

You can count on it, Josh thought to himself with a masculine smile of anticipation. *And you're going to be enjoying it with me, Pam. Enjoying it very much!*

CHAPTER TWO

Pam woke up the next morning feeling like a new woman. The hot bath she'd soaked in the night before had helped to soothe away the aches and pains left from her accident. Her optimism restored, she was ready to face the world, and to locate the man she'd come to Bermuda to find — her boss, Roger Bass.

Sitting up in bed, Pam wrapped her arms around her knees and took a moment to review her predicament. She still found it hard to believe that Roger had actually taken off with their clients' money! He wasn't that kind of man.

But then Roger hadn't been himself lately; he'd been increasingly depressed over his approaching fiftieth birthday. As the owner of Global Travel Agency in Chicago and a widower for five years, Roger had dealt with stress before. He'd always been responsible, always been dependable, and he'd never missed a day of work. But two days ago Roger hadn't shown up at the agency. He hadn't been at home either.

A search through Roger's infamously chaotic desk hadn't unearthed any explanatory note. Instead two disturbing facts had been uncovered. The money box that should have contained the deposits made the previous day by clients was empty — except for a crumpled carbon of a ticket in Roger's name. The destination was Bermuda. Pam had viewed the carbon as a good sign. She believed Roger had deliberately left a clue so that someone would follow him and stop him.

It only made sense that Pam would be that someone. Roger had been there for her when she'd needed help. Her life hadn't exactly been filled with prospects when she'd walked into his travel agency in answer to a help-wanted ad. The ad had clearly stated that previous experience was a prerequisite. It wasn't the first such ad she'd run across. But as she'd so vehemently pointed out to Roger some six years ago, how was she supposed to get experience if someone wouldn't give her a chance?

Roger had given her that chance, and Pam never forgot it. Now it was her turn to repay him. She had to find him before the loss at the agency came to light. Pam had sworn her fellow travel agent, Anita Brankowski, to secrecy and instructed her to hold down the fort until Pam brought back Roger — and the money.

As if induced by her thoughts of home, the

phone in Pam's small room rang. It was Anita.

"Have you come up with anything yet?" the young woman asked. Anita was someone else Roger had helped. She'd been in the process of going through a painful divorce when Roger hired her.

"Not yet," Pam replied. "I told you I'd give you a call the minute I found anything."

"I know you did." Anita's voice faltered. "I couldn't wait any longer. I'm sorry."

"That's okay. I know it's hard on you, being there on your own. But you can do it, Anita," Pam reassured her. "I know you can. Everything will be all right. Keep telling yourself that."

"I do," Anita answered. "The trouble is believing it."

"Roger believed in you, Anita. He believed in me too. Now it's time for us to believe in him."

"I do believe in him, and I can't believe he's done this."

"I know," Pam acknowledged. "Listen, the minute I know something, I'll give you a call."

"Pam, do you think you could call me tonight with a status report? Waiting around for the phone to ring is driving me crazy," Anita confessed with a nervous laugh.

"Sure, I can do that. Don't worry, Anita. I'll find him."

Pam began her search by calling all the main resorts listed in a booklet she'd pulled from the travel agency's files. The information was put together by the Bermuda Department of Tourism and was up to date. Unfortunately none of the nine resorts she called had anyone registered named Roger Bass.

Even so, Pam refused to let herself become discouraged. She began dialing the dozen or so smaller hotels, then the guest houses, then the housekeeping cottages and apartments, until she'd phoned every accommodation listed. Still no luck. No one had heard of Roger Bass.

Roger must be registered under an alias. Either that or he was staying in an unlisted rental property. The first possibility would be easier to follow than the second, so she went with that one. Thank goodness she'd brought a photograph of Roger with her. She'd show it around and see if anyone recognized him. Going downstairs, she started with the registration desk of her own resort.

"Excuse me, I wonder if you could tell me if you've seen this man?" she asked the young woman at the desk. "He's a friend of mine and it's possible that he might be staying here."

Pam repeated her question to the concierge, the restaurant's head waiter, the bellman. The answer was always the same. No one had seen Roger.

But Pam had seen Josh Phillips. He was watching her, and she didn't appreciate it. She tried ignoring him, but knew that wouldn't last long. She was right. Josh approached her just as she'd finished speaking to her last interviewee.

"Good morning, Pam." His voice was low and outrageously intimate. "No bad after-effects from our little run in yesterday, I see."

Josh Phillips saw entirely too much, Pam decided. For one thing, he was looking at her as if visually undressing her. Her khaki slacks and tropical-print shirt proved to be an ineffectual barrier to his provocative stare. Pam had to fight the inclination to look down and make sure that everything was buttoned and fastened properly. It was hard, though. Real hard.

"Excuse me," she said in what she hoped was a crisp tone. "I was just on my way out."

"Out where? Not trying to rent another moped, I hope." He held up his hands as if preparing to ward off her protests. "I'm not prying," he mockingly assured her. "I just want to make sure that it's safe for me to jog along the road without being knocked over."

"If you want to be safe you should stick to the beach," Pam retorted. "Or use the health spa here at the resort."

"Danger must appeal to me." *You appeal to me,* his devilish eyes told her.

Forget it, her eyes angrily flashed back. "Danger doesn't appeal to me at all."

"Really? I find that hard to believe."

Pam was well aware that their discussion was being held on two levels. "Believe what you like, facts are facts. As I said, I'm on my way out."

"Ah yes, still in search of the elusive Roger, I see."

The mockery in his voice aroused her anger. So Josh found her amusing, did he? "I seem to recall your saying that you were here in Bermuda on vacation, Josh. So feel free to go vacate!"

"*Free* does not describe the way I feel when I'm around you. *Frustrated, intrigued* and *aroused* come closer to the truth — although not necessarily in that order!"

Pam didn't know how to respond to that, and it threw her. Josh threw her.

And he knew it. He saw it in her dark eyes. He wanted her and he made sure she knew it. He knew that Pam wasn't prepared to admit that the feeling was reciprocated, but she would. He knew she would.

Pam's eyes narrowed suspiciously. *Oh, no you don't. Not me. I'm not falling for that boyish charm. You may be a man used to getting your own way, but you're going to have to get it with someone else.* A shake of her head added emphasis to her thoughts.

Josh fanned the fire of her anger by nodding. *Yes, you,* he seemed to be saying.

Pam refused to continue standing in the lobby swapping thoughts back and forth with a man who had no intention of listening to her anyway. Without saying another word, she stalked outside.

Luck was with her, for a change. A cab had just pulled up. The moment the occupants had unloaded, she got inside and told the driver to take her to a neighboring resort. To her surprise, the driver was Trevor.

"You're alone today?" he questioned.

"Yes, thank heavens."

Trevor shook his head. "That's too bad," he said as he drove out of the resort's long and winding entryway. "What happened to your fellow?"

"Josh is not my fellow and nothing's happened to him — yet," Pam added under her breath. She was tempted to do Josh some bodily harm herself. Who did he think he was, eyeing her like that? Not that she was a prude;

she was accustomed to receiving her fair share of masculine stares, but none had been so. . . . *So what?* she asked herself. *So effective? So arousing?*

It didn't matter; she didn't have time to analyze her reaction to Josh Phillips. She had more important things to take care of than wondering about some man, attractive though he might be. She had to find Roger before he spent all their clients' money. If she didn't, she and Anita could both be charged as accessories to the crime, since they hadn't reported the missing money to the authorities.

Trevor was chatting about the good weather and the need for rain as he stopped the cab in front of the main entrance of the very ritzy hotel.

Before getting out, Pam leaned forward to show Roger's photograph to Trevor. "Have you seen this man? He's a friend of mine who's staying here in Bermuda and I'm trying to find him. His name is Roger Bass."

Trevor took the photograph and studied it before handing it back to Pam. "I haven't seen him. Your other fellow looks much better, though. This one's too old for you."

Pam gritted her teeth and counted to ten. "Josh is not my fellow, and neither is Roger. He's just a friend."

"Josh is just a friend?" Trevor asked.

"No, Roger is just a friend."

"And Josh?"

"Forget Josh!" Pam was getting exasperated and she made no attempt to hide it. "This is important, Trevor. If you should see Roger, would you give me a call? You know where I'm staying."

Trevor nodded. "The same place Josh is staying."

With that, Pam gave up on Trevor.

She had no luck questioning the employees at the hotel or at the dozen other South Shore resorts she tried. Pam returned to her own hotel feeling disheartened. She had gotten one small lead, though. The receptionist at the last hotel she'd stopped at had suggested checking the public beaches a short distance away. "Sooner or later, everyone shows up at the beaches," the woman told her. "Nobody can resist them!"

As far as Pam knew, Roger had no great liking for pink beaches, lovely though they might be. But the woman had gone on to say that travel experts rated Bermuda's beaches as among the ten most beautiful in the world. Roger was a travel expert, wasn't he? Maybe he was checking out the beaches.

Pam stopped by her room just long enough to pick up the red one-piece swimsuit she'd brought with her. She was too nervous to eat lunch, so she added a few oranges to the sunglasses and bottle of suntan oil she'd already tossed into a straw bag.

Pam chose to go to Horseshoe Bay because it was one of the largest and reputed to be one of the most spectacular of the public beaches. It was also one of the closest.

Horseshoe Bay lived up to its reputation. Upset though she was, Pam took a moment to let the beauty of the scenery sink in. The woman at the hotel hadn't been exaggerating when she'd said the beaches were pink. The sand beneath Pam's bare feet was powder soft and delicately tinged with color, making the contrast between it and the brilliant azure water all the more spectacular.

Pam had already used the changing rooms to slip into her swimsuit. The beach was very crowded, with people of all ages enjoying the sunshine and the ocean. Pam strolled through the crowds, as if looking for the perfect spot to lie down and soak up some sun. In fact, she was searching the multitude of faces for one in particular — Roger's. *You'd think his red hair would make him easy to find,* she thought to herself, although as Roger had often complained lately, that red hair was rapidly thinning. *Still, he shouldn't be too hard to spot.*

So Pam continued to make her way along the beach. She began at the back and worked her way closer and closer to the water. She passed family outings, honeymooning couples and snoozing sun worshippers. She heard crisp English accents and the gentle rhythm of Bermudian voices. And from a heated game of volleyball taking place on one side of the beach, she heard the loud, exuberant voices of her fellow Americans.

A short distance away a mother and father were trying to coax their young daughter to get her feet wet in the temperate surf. Pam stood and watched as the little girl fearfully clutched her parents' hands. She was particularly struck by the father's gentle patience and understanding — he didn't force his daughter into the water; he waited until she was ready. What a difference from her own childhood, Pam thought, remembering the time when her adoptive father had taken her to one of Chicago's beaches. With her it had been a case of sink or swim. There had been nothing patient or gentle about it.

Distracted as she was by her thoughts, Pam was unaware that the neighboring volleyball game had broken up as the college-age participants reverted to horseplay. The young women shrieked as their boyfriends grabbed them and ran with them toward the ocean, where they made a big production out of dumping them into the water. Pam was concerned about the little girl's proximity to the cavorting bunch and paid no heed to her own nearness to the group. She was relieved to see the father scoop his daughter up in his arms and return her to the safety of their beach blanket.

The same could not be said of Pam. While she'd been standing there, the group of students had gotten closer and closer until they were now surrounding her. She was about to turn and resume her search for Roger when she was suddenly grabbed from behind and tossed over some joker's shoulder. With a whooping varsity cry she was carried out to the water and unceremoniously dropped in.

It happened so quickly that Pam, whose mouth was open to voice a violent protest, ended up getting a mouthful of saltwater instead. The water was deeper than she'd expected, and she found herself floundering as she tried to get some air into her oxygen-starved lungs.

Josh saw her sputtering and didn't think twice about practicing his lifeguard routine on her. He'd been watching her — had, in fact, followed her to the beach and had been about to approach her when that beach bum with the University of Miami T-shirt intervened. Josh felt an overwhelming urge to punch the idiot, but first he had to rescue Pam.

When Pam felt a pair of hands on her, she reacted instinctively. Disgusted with the jerk who'd dumped her in the water, she kicked out. If he touched her again, she'd cripple him!

"Calm down, I've got you," a masculine voice muttered in her ear as she furiously treaded water. "It's Josh."

Before she could make any kind of response, Josh had turned her onto her back and was towing her ashore. As soon as they reached shallow water, he stood with her in his arms and carried her to the blanket he'd left spread out on the sand.

Pam was still sputtering, this time from fury.

"You seem to be having some trouble catching your breath," Josh murmured as he knelt beside her. "Maybe I can help."

Droplets of water fell from his face onto hers as he moved even closer. A second later his lips touched hers in a teasing parody of mouth-to-mouth resuscitation.

As Josh explored the soft curves of her lips, Pam hazily realized that she should be fighting him off. But she couldn't seem to get her hands to push him away. She was frozen by her conflicting desires while Josh's gentle assault on her senses completely undermined her better judgment.

Shaken by her feelings, Pam closed her eyes to savor the taste and texture of his mouth. His tongue daringly circled her lower lip, sampling the delicacy of her vulnerable flesh. Her gasps of pleasure were consumed by him as he once again brushed his mouth across hers.

Just as he'd planned, Josh's restraint quickly enticed her into his web. Logical thought disappeared, and Pam forgot all the reasons for staying away from Josh. She forgot everything but the feel of his arms around her, of his mouth seducing hers. She wanted more.

She got it. Tasting success, Josh immediately increased the intensity of his kisses. While before his lips had playfully toyed with hers, now his mouth possessed hers. The progression from teasing temptation to hungry seduction was swift and intoxicating.

Pam trembled with excitement. Her heart was racing wildly as Josh drew her more deeply into his embrace. He held her so close that she could feel everything about him. The warmth of his bare chest burned through the thin sleekness of her swimsuit.

When Josh lightly brushed the side of her breast with his fingertips, Pam realized that her self-control was slipping out of her hands and into his. She recognized the danger immediately. Finally her hands listened and obeyed her mental commands to push Josh away instead of pull him closer.

Her efforts to get free were assisted by the sound of someone's voice saying, "Is she all right?"

Reluctantly Josh let her go and turned to glare at the beach jock who'd dropped Pam into the ocean in the first place.

The burning anger in Josh's eyes made the young man take several steps backward. "I'm real sorry," he stuttered. "I thought she was my girlfriend. They've both got dark hair, y'know? And she was standing right where I thought Buffy was." The college student shifted nervously. "I didn't mean to grab your girl like that. No hard feelings, huh?"

"Just don't come near her again," Josh retorted angrily.

"No problem, no problem," the young man assured him.

"Idiot," Josh muttered as the college student made a hasty getaway.

As far as Pam was concerned, Josh and the college student who'd dunked her were both idiots. "Let go of me!" she demanded in a furious tone of voice. She jerked away from Josh.

He looked at her with that devilish gleam in his blue eyes. "I save your life and this is the thanks I get for it?"

"You didn't save my life," she countered. "I know how to swim."

"It didn't look like it to me. You were floundering out there. That's not the way most people swim. Besides, Doc told you to keep your arm dry until it healed completely."

Pam was stung more by his uncomplimentary description of her aquatic talents than by his reminder of her medical orders. "I'll have you know that I've won several awards for my swimming."

"Awards?" Josh laughed and shook his head. "For what? Having the most unusual . . . stroke?"

He drawled that last word, intentionally reminding her of intimacies so recently shared. There was no doubt about it, Josh Phillips was a master at the game between the sexes — a game Pam had no intention of playing. Not with him.

Kissing him had been an alarming revelation. He'd taken control of her emotions, and being controlled was something Pam refused to permit. Never again.

Having settled that issue within her own mind, Pam prepared to get up and get away from Josh Phillips without further delay.

As he'd done the first time they met, Josh clamped a restraining hand around her leg to prevent her from leaving. Pam resented it now even more than she had before. Because now she knew how dangerous Josh really was.

"Just stay put for a minute," he told her. "We're not done talking yet."

"Yes, we are." She was tempted to add that he never talked anyway, he only made pronouncements. But she had no intention of getting into an argument with him. He had baited her so that she'd react and she was determined not to fall for that routine again.

Josh, however, was equally determined. "This afternoon's incident at the beach has made something very clear to me." Her mutinous expression made him smile. "You obviously need someone to keep you out of trouble."

Pam saw red. "Stop right there. I don't need anyone to keep me out of trouble. I'm perfectly capable of taking care of myself. I've been doing it for some time now."

"You haven't been doing a very good job at it," he retorted. "In the two days I've known you, you've already gotten yourself nearly killed twice. Yesterday you crashed your moped and today you almost drowned."

"How many times do I have to tell you that I didn't almost drown?" Pam exclaimed, infuriated by his biased reporting of the facts. "I was just caught by surprise, that's all. I was perfectly capable of getting to shore by myself, without your lifeguard routine. And as for yesterday's crash — if you hadn't been jogging along the road, I would have had plenty of room to come to a safe stop. I only crashed the moped to avoid hitting you."

"Leave it to a woman to put the blame on the man," Josh murmured.

"That does it!" Pam broke away from him and scrambled to her feet with more haste than grace. "There's no use talking with you. Just do me a favor and stay away from me. I don't need your help and I don't need you."

"Funny, that's not what your kiss said," he taunted.

His inflammatory comment stopped her in her tracks, just as he'd meant it to. "My kiss didn't say anything," she shot back. "Kisses can't talk. But *I* can, and you'd better listen to what I'm saying."

"I would listen if I thought what you're saying was the truth," Josh calmly replied. "But I don't believe that. I believe you felt the same attraction I did. That kiss we shared proved it. You may be afraid to admit it, but that doesn't change things. The fact is, you're as attracted to me as I am to you, and I'm not about to let your obstinacy stand in the way."

Her obstinacy? What about his pigheadedness? Pam was so furious she was shaking. Who did Josh Phillips think he was? "You're crazy," she stated angrily. "I don't need a keeper, I don't need anyone!"

Pam repeated those words to herself as she marched to the changing room. What she *needed* was to find Roger, and to stay away from Josh Phillips!

CHAPTER THREE

Staying away from Josh was easier said than done, as Pam discovered when she entered the resort's dining room later that evening.

"I'd like a table for one, please," she told the maître d'.

"Your name?"

Although she was somewhat surprised by the request, Pam gave him her name. She hadn't made a reservation, so she didn't know why the maître d' needed it — unless he'd wanted to check to make sure she was a guest?

Pam looked down at her dark rose-color skirt and matching knit top with a frown. She was aware that due to its British heritage, Bermuda's dress code was somewhat conservative, which was why she'd made a point of changing for dinner. So her pearl necklace and earrings were fake; was that any reason to look at her so strangely and question her suitability as a guest?

Pam was about to confront the maître d' when she was distracted by a more immediate problem. The table to which she was being led was already occupied — by Josh.

Pam grabbed hold of the maître d's arm to

get his attention. "Excuse me, you must have misunderstood me. I requested a table for one."

"I know you did. This is the only table for one we have left."

The table was set so close to Josh's table that the two of them might as well have been sitting together.

Well aware of her thoughts, Josh said, "You're welcome to join me at my table. We're practically sharing anyway."

"No, thank you." Pam's voice may have been polite, but her expression was remote. She had no doubt that Josh had arranged this little maneuver with the maître d'. "I prefer to sit alone."

"Suit yourself." Josh shrugged as if her refusal were of no importance to him.

Pam chose to sit facing Josh, rather than sitting right beside him. In more ways than one, it was like choosing between a rock and a hard place. This way she was at the mercy of Josh's deep blue eyes. He was looking at her in a way that was infinitely disturbing. His gaze held a mixture of knowledge and amusement — as if he were capable of reading her thoughts; as if he wanted her to read his.

Pam used her own eyes to tell him that she already knew what he was thinking and she wasn't interested. She then opened the oversize menu and held it up, effectively blocking Josh's visual seduction. Taking a deep breath, she attempted to recover her equilibrium.

"Your menu is upside down," Josh murmured dryly. "If you're having trouble deciding, I can recommend the seafood."

"I'm allergic to seafood," Pam replied, without lowering her menu. She did turn it right-side up, however.

"Too bad. You're missing a great deal of satisfaction."

Before Pam could reply to his outrageous statement, Josh had already gone on to a more prosaic subject. "You never told me what happened with your moped. Did the rental agency give you any trouble after it was returned?"

Pam was tempted to ignore his question but decided that to do so would be to play right into his hands. He only said the outrageous things he did so that she'd make some kind of reply. Maybe the best way of dealing with Josh was to use polite conversation. "I'd taken out insurance, so there was no problem. I don't think they're eager for me to rent another moped, however."

"I can't blame them," Josh said.

Pam stifled her anger and decided to turn the tables on him. This time she'd be the one asking questions. "What are you doing here in

Bermuda — aside from bothering me, that is?"

"Ah, so I *am* bothering you! You finally admit it."

The man was impossible. "What made you choose Bermuda for your vacation?" Pam asked in her best travel agent voice.

"I've been here before and enjoyed it. I needed a break between business meetings in Mexico and the Middle East, and this fit the geographical bill to a tee."

"You're a businessman?"

"You sound surprised."

"I am," she acknowledged. "You don't seem the three-piece-suit type to me."

"I'm not. I'm an engineer. I happened to hit it lucky developing a better mousetrap, or in this case a better coupling connector for the pipes used in oil fields. Thanks to the patent I hold on that, I've been able to go into business for myself."

So Josh was an engineer. He'd certainly managed to engineer more than his fair share of events with her. And somehow it came as no surprise to hear that he was involved in the rough-and-tumble world of oil fields, or that he was an apparent expert on coupling!

"How about you?" Josh questioned as he watched the play of emotions reflected in her eyes. "What do you do, when you're not knocking innocent men off their feet?"

"I doubt if you were ever innocent," Pam retorted before answering. "I'm a travel agent."

"That's why you're here in Bermuda on business?"

"You could say that." However, if she didn't find Roger soon, the chances of her still being in business were slim. Most of the money Roger had embezzled belonged to her clients, and she knew they would hold her personally responsible for the loss of their deposits. Suddenly she wasn't as hungry as she'd thought. "I'll just have the chef's salad and a glass of iced tea," she told the waiter.

"That's not enough to eat for dinner," Josh said. "If you're on a diet, there's no need." He paused to give her an intimate once-over. "Remember, I've seen you in a swimsuit and I can vouch for the fact that you're perfect just the way you are."

Pam couldn't help but be complimented, until she reminded herself that the comment was just another of Josh's smooth lines. "I'm not on a diet, I'm just not very hungry."

"Crashing mopeds and almost drowning can be hard on the system," Josh said with mocking commiseration.

"Don't get started on that again," Pam warned him. "How old are you?"

Josh looked surprised by her non sequitur. "Thirty-three. Why?"

"If you want to live to be thirty-four then you'd better not mention mopeds or drowning again," she answered. "You savvy?"

Josh leaned back and looked at her with mocking admiration. "Feisty little thing, aren't you?"

"Spunky big thing, aren't you?" she shot back. "And for your information, five feet five inches is not little."

"Compared to my six foot one, it is," he retorted.

Pam didn't want to compare herself to him; she was in enough trouble already. So far she'd been able to keep thoughts of Josh's well-developed body at bay. But it hadn't been easy. Memories of him carrying her out of the water kept filtering through her defenses. At least when he'd picked her up after the moped accident he'd been wearing some sort of top, even if it had been an abbreviated one. But at the beach he'd only been wearing a pair of black swim trunks. Her fingertips tingled with the remembered warmth of his bare skin. He'd been tan all over, no doubt thanks to his time spent working in the oil fields.

Pam's evocative reverie was interrupted by the arrival of their waiter, who carried Josh's dinner on the same tray as Pam's chef's salad.

She had to admit that Josh's plate full of scallops did look good. She wasn't really allergic to seafood; she'd only said that to provoke him.

When Josh caught her eyeing his dinner he speared several plump scallops and held out his fork invitingly. "Want to taste one?" he asked her.

Although she was tempted to say yes, Pam shook her head.

"Sure? Not even one taste?" he coaxed enticingly. "You never know, you might like it and discover that you want more." As he spoke, Josh was looking at her mouth with wicked deliberation, reminding her of the kiss they'd shared on the beach and offering her the promise of many more in the future.

It was an offer Pam refused.

Josh was not discouraged. He hadn't expected her to accept. But he'd accomplished what he intended: a flash of recognition between them. He'd seen it in her eyes. She hadn't forgotten their kiss, much as she might have wanted to.

Pam stoically ate her salad and tried to keep her eyes away from Josh. He had the look of a rogue tonight, even more so than normal. She couldn't exactly put her finger on what it was about him; the elegant evening clothes or the experienced gleam in his eye. She only knew that he bothered her in a way that was unsettling.

That being the case, she finished her meal as quickly as possible. Pam tried telling herself that she was in a hurry because she had to get on with the search for Roger, but she had to admit that Josh's proximity and frequent glances played a large part in her decision.

"Leaving so early?" Josh commented after Pam had asked the waiter for the check.

"That's right." She stood and looked down at him with hard-won composure. "I've got a lot to do."

Josh frowned at her departing figure. He didn't like the sound of her last words. He had a feeling they meant she was resuming her search for Roger Bass. He'd never met a woman who got into so much trouble with so little effort. He'd never met a woman like Pam Warner, period. Swearing softly, Josh caught the waiter's attention and got his own check.

Upstairs in her room, Pam was placing a long distance call to Anita back in Chicago.

"No news yet," she told Anita. "I'm just on my way out now to check a few of the nightspots and see if I can find Roger there. How did things go at the agency today?"

"No problems yet."

"That's good news." Between Roger's disappearance and Josh's sensual pursuit, Pam had enough problems as it was. She arranged to call Anita again the next night, or sooner if she found Roger. Then she slipped on a white linen jacket and walked out of her room.

Pam took a taxi to the closest, and only, nightclub near the South Shore hotels. Dancing had just begun at nine, and the place was hopping. It was difficult talking over the loud music, but Pam managed it. With a wine spritzer in one hand and Roger's photo in the other, she made the rounds of the club's patrons. She hadn't really expected to find anything at her first stop, so she wasn't too disappointed when no one recognized Roger.

Another taxi took her into Hamilton, where there were half a dozen more nightspots for her to check out. She'd switched from wine to ginger ale after her second stop. There was no point in getting tipsy, and it looked like it was going to be a long night.

During the next few hours Pam heard calypso music, watched large-screen rock videos, and danced to a steel-band version of Gershwin's "Rhapsody in Blue." She asked everyone she met if they'd seen Roger. Her questioning involved her in some curious conversations.

"Are you with the police?" an insurance broker from New York City asked her.

His companion, a stewardess, was looking at Pam warily. They were all sharing a table to watch a limbo show.

"No, I'm just trying to find him for personal reasons," Pam answered. "Nothing to do with the police." And she prayed it would stay that way.

"Why are you looking for him?" a woman bartender asked her at another club. "Has he done something illegal?"

Pam wasn't sure how to answer that one. Technically what Roger had done was illegal, but it wasn't really a reported crime yet. So she compromised by saying, "I'm afraid he might get into trouble."

"I'll keep my eyes open for him," the woman promised.

"Thanks, I'd appreciate it." Pam gave the woman the name of the hotel where she was staying.

"Has he been missing long?" a newlywed couple asked Pam. "Is he one of those missing people you hear about?"

"I hope not," Pam muttered wearily.

By the time Pam entered the last nightclub it was well after midnight. She wasn't in the best of moods, and the thick cloud of cigarette smoke hanging in the air made her eyes water. The place was crowded, with a higher percentage of men than women. Pam's throat had long since grown raspy from trying to make herself heard over the variety of musical entertainment. Her presentation had been shortened accordingly so that it now only contained the necessary information.

She began by saying, "Excuse me, I'm looking for a man —"

She was interrupted by a burly guy at the bar who lurched forward and slurred, "You've foun' 'im, honey!" His hand shot out, stopping Pam's instinctive movement of escape. Thick stubby fingers closed around her upper arm with sickening strength.

Pam reacted to the unwanted physical restraint with impatient fury. She'd already had to stomach too many sexual innuendoes and lecherous passes for one evening. "Listen, you lounge lizard, get your crummy hands off me!"

It was the wrong approach to take. She became aware of that immediately. The man grew even more belligerent. Pressing oppressively closer, he began muttering obscenities into her ear. His panting breath repelled her. Pam struggled to get free, but the man easily weighed twice as much as she did and he was not about to release her. She'd just lifted her knee in a last resort self-protection measure when she was freed so abruptly she stumbled and almost fell.

"The lady doesn't want to be bothered," she heard Josh growl menacingly. "You got that?"

Pam stared at Josh with startled eyes. She was shocked, as much by the primitive violence in his face as by his unexpected appearance. He was gripping the lounge lizard's shirt front so tightly that the collar was cutting off the man's blood supply and turning his face purple.

"You got that?" Josh repeated, shaking the burly man as if he were a flyweight.

Panic-stricken, the drunk nodded.

Only then did Josh release him.

Pam still stood staring at Josh. What was he doing here? And what had happened to the mocking rogue she'd left after dinner? The Josh who turned to face her was a ruthless man who was so angry she could practically feel the waves of fury emanating from him. That fury was now being directed toward her.

"Of all the lame-brain, simple-minded, idiotic stunts to pull! Come on, let's get out of here." He dragged her from the club to a waiting taxi parked outside.

"What are you doing?" Pam protested as Josh practically shoved her into the back of the taxi.

Josh got in right behind her and slammed the door with a force that made the entire taxi shake. "Lady, if you know what's good for you, you'll just sit there and keep your mouth shut. In case you hadn't noticed, I'm not in the best of moods at the moment."

"Neither am I," she retorted. "But that's no reason to drag me out of the bar. Why are you mad at me? That scene back there wasn't my fault."

"Wait till we get back to the hotel," he curtly ordered.

Pam did wait, but only long enough for the cab to pull to a stop outside their resort. Without saying a word to Josh, she shoved open the cab door and dashed into the lobby. She slid between the closing doors of an elevator just in the nick of time.

Pam was positively fuming. Instead of finding Roger, she'd almost ended up in the middle of a bar-room brawl. And to top it all off, for some unknown reason Josh had decided to place all the blame on her. How like a man!

Pam had her key out of her purse and ready to insert into her door lock when she got off the elevator. She almost made it, too. Then, just as she was about to turn the key, Josh appeared at her side.

"Going somewhere?" he inquired with ominous softness.

"Obviously." Pam turned to give him a

coolly dismissive look. "This is my room."

"Fine. I'll join you." Josh turned the key, opened the door and hauled her inside.

Pam tugged her arm away from his angry grasp. Her eyes were shooting fire as she glared at him. "Listen, buddy, I'm getting real tired of being dragged around like this. I don't know what your problem is —"

He tossed his jacket onto her bed and peremptorily interrupted her. "My problem is you and your stupid search."

"I don't know what you're talking about!" Pam shouted. "And what's more, I don't care. You can go rant and rave someplace else. I want you out of my room, now!"

"You got the first part of that right." Josh's voice lowered with unmistakable intent. "You do want me."

If Pam had thought Josh dangerous before, he was even more so now. He had the unmistakable air of a predator.

"You're crazy, do you know that?" Pam's voice rose. "First you haul me out of the nightclub in Hamilton and now you practically break into my room and inform me that I want you. Not exactly the behavior of a sane man, if you ask me."

Josh's anger resurfaced. "And I suppose chasing after a man who obviously doesn't want to be found is sane behavior? What does it take to get through to you? It's obvious that Bass isn't interested in you anymore. So why do you persist in this stupid search?"

"I told you before, that's none of your business."

"I'm making it my business," he told her.

"Tough!"

"That's what you'd like me to think, isn't it? That you're a tough lady capable of taking care of yourself." Josh's voice lowered again. "But you weren't very capable in that bar tonight, were you? Do you know what could have happened to you if I hadn't shown up when I did?"

"Nothing would have happened," Pam retorted. "I would have gotten rid of the jerk. I do know some self-defense, you know."

Josh started closing in on her. "The same way you know how to swim and how to drive?"

He'd removed his tie and unbuttoned the first few buttons of his shirt. His light brown hair fell recklessly across his forehead, the sun-lightened streaks even more evident in the soft lighting of her room. He looked sexier at that moment than any man she'd seen. Pam knew she had to get him out of her room. And fast!

"This discussion is over," she stated. "If you don't leave immediately I'm going to call the front desk and have you thrown out."

Josh did not look at all perturbed by her threat. "Rule number one, Pam. Never tell the opposition your game plan. It takes away the element of surprise."

"I'll remember that if I should ever find myself having to deal with a crazy man again," she noted sarcastically. "But I don't think the situation will ever recur. I make it a point to avoid men like you."

This time her taunt did get to him. "You prefer to spend all your time chasing men like Bass?"

"Roger is worth ten of you!" Pam hurled the words at him.

"We'll see about that." Josh snared her in his arms. "Stop wasting your time on Bass. He may not want you, but I sure as hell do!"

CHAPTER FOUR

Josh didn't waste any more words trying to prove that he wanted Pam. Instead he swiftly covered her mouth with his own, stifling the sharp retort she was about to make.

This time there was no preliminary teasing as there had been when he'd kissed her on the beach. This time his mouth engulfed hers, the slant and angle such that there was no denying the hungry intimacy.

His intention was clear. Josh wanted her to admit she desired him as much as he desired her. Pam struggled to retain control, but it was a losing battle. Her lips were easily persuaded to open for him. When his tongue erotically dipped inside to stroke the warm depths of her mouth, she knew it was hopeless. Pleasure this strong wasn't meant to be fought.

Josh was aware of the exact moment that her angry resistance became yielding compliance. Now that they were both equal partners in the kiss, their mouths merged with consuming fire. Passion prevailed as Josh pulled her even closer, making her a prisoner of her own desire.

Heedless of the danger of her actions, Pam ran her fingers over Josh's broad shoulders, savoring the warmth of his skin beneath the thin cotton of his shirt. He felt so solid and muscular that she was tempted to widen her explorations, traveling from his shoulders around to his back. She slid her fingers down his spine, relishing the freedom to touch him as she pleased.

Josh was already touching her, caressing her. His hands slipped beneath the knit material of her top to stroke her bare skin. His touch was firm and sure as he blazed a seductive trail around the curve of her waist.

From there it was only a matter of seconds before his hand spanned the short distance to her breast. But in those brief seconds time seemed to stand still. Pam shivered with anticipation, knowing what was coming and uncertain if she could stand the suspense a moment longer.

Josh moved in swiftly, seductively. He began by stroking the underside of her breast with his index finger before moving his entire hand up to claim her. Heated excitement coursed through her, blotting out all rational thought.

Josh allowed her gasps of pleasure to punctuate their kisses as he continued to caress her breasts with devilish expertise; holding her, manipulating her. The sheer intensity of her pleasure shocked her, causing her to move against him. Now that her hips were pressed intimately against his, she could feel the strength of his arousal.

"Don't tell me that Bass ever made you feel this way," Josh murmured seductively against her ear.

The sound of Roger's name brought Pam to her senses with stunning abruptness. Despite what they'd just shared, Josh still thought that she and Roger were intimately involved. Josh had only kissed her, caressed her, to stake his own claim! Pam was furious, both at herself for responding to Josh and at him for misreading the situation.

She shoved an angry hand at Josh's unyielding shoulder in an attempt to free herself from his hold. It was useless. He was as immovable as the Rock of Gibraltar.

Pam's anger flared. "You men are all alike! You all have one-track minds. I'm fed up with it, do you hear me? You're as bad as that lounge lizard in the bar!" She punctuated each sentence with a sock to Josh's arm.

Startled by her attack, Josh tightened his grip on her, pinning her arms to her side so she couldn't keep hitting him. "Stop that!"

Restrained once again, Pam resorted to the truth. She shouted it out loud. "Roger isn't my boyfriend, and he isn't my lover! He's my employer, and he's in big trouble. We're both in big trouble." Tears of anger, anxiety and frustration filled her eyes and rolled down her face. "Now look what you've done!" she practically wailed. "You've made me cry, and I never cry!"

Josh coped well with having a wild woman in his arms. His embrace softened as he added soothing strokes down her back.

"It'd serve you right if I get your shirt all wet," Pam muttered unsteadily.

"Go right ahead," he invited her. "I get the impression this crying jag's been a long time coming." Anchoring his hand at the nape of her neck, he rubbed his thumb along the taut muscles.

"Being nice isn't going to change things." Her words were interspersed with sniffs. "I'm still mad at you and I still want you to let me go."

"I'll let you go in a minute," he promised. "As soon as you're done crying."

Pam drew in a deep breath before announcing, "I'm done now."

"Come sit down." Josh led her to a chair near the window and lowered her into the welcome softness. Then he pulled a handful of tissues from a box on the table. "Here." He crouched beside her and handed her a tissue.

"Now, tell me, what kind of trouble are you in? And don't bother saying it's none of my business, Pam. I want to help you."

"I know what you want, and helping me has nothing to do with it," Pam retorted.

Josh grinned at her restored spunkiness. "I want you, I don't deny that. But I also want to help you."

Pam stopped wiping her tears long enough to give him a suspicious look. "Why should I believe you?"

"Because you want to find Bass and you haven't had any luck doing it alone." He paused as if daring her to deny that fact. When she didn't, he resumed his questioning. "Now tell me, why are you looking for him?"

"If I tell you — and I'm not saying I will — you've got to promise me that you won't go to the police."

Josh gave her a narrow-eyed stare that would have made a weaker woman give in. "Just what exactly have you gotten yourself involved with?"

Typically, Pam reacted to the intimidation with impatience, not fear. "Stop looking at me like that — it's nothing illegal." She thought a second and then revised her statement. "Well, maybe it is illegal, but it's just a misunderstanding. I don't want the law involved in this because a man's reputation is at stake, not to mention my job."

Josh didn't say anything; he just looked at her with inflexible persistence. For some reason Pam trusted him. And she suspected that having him on her side was better than fighting him all the time. So she finally decided to confide in Josh.

"Roger is my employer; he owns the travel agency where I work. Last Wednesday Roger didn't show up at the office. He didn't call in, either. We got worried, Anita and I. Anita is another travel agent who works with me," she explained. "Anyway, Roger had never skipped a day of work before, not without calling in sick or something. So we checked Roger's desk to see if he'd left a note. We didn't find any note but we did find an empty cash box."

Josh frowned. "Why didn't you report this to the police?"

"Because Roger isn't the kind of man who would embezzle his clients' money."

"It sounds like he did just that," Josh pointed out.

"You don't understand. Roger was upset about his birthday — he'll be turning fifty at the end of the month. He's in mid-life crisis. He just took off in a moment of madness."

"Since Roger has been missing for almost three days now, I'd say it was more than just a moment of madness."

Pam ignored Josh's mocking observation. "I know that if I could just talk to him, I could convince Roger to come back."

Her comment erased the humor from Josh's face and replaced it with disbelief. "Are you nuts? You seriously believe that a man who's embezzled money is going to turn around and return it just because you ask him to?"

"I told you, Roger Bass isn't that kind of man. For the past six years he's been my mentor; he gave me a chance to prove myself when no one else would. I'm telling you, I know the man!"

Seeing that she was upset, Josh deliberately spoke in a soothing voice. "Pam, you're not in any position to judge this situation objectively."

But his attitude only irritated her more. "I'm not being blindly emotional, I'm being practical. The fact that I know Roger gives me an advantage over the police — I've got a better chance of finding him than they have."

"What makes you think Roger came to Bermuda?"

"He left a copy of his ticket in the cash box," she replied, as if pulling a rabbit out of a hat. "So you see, Roger does want me to find him."

Josh was not at all convinced. "It could just have been carelessness on his part."

Pam didn't let Josh's pessimism depress her. "I have to find Roger before he spends too much of our clients' money."

"Going around the island by yourself showing people a picture of Roger isn't going to do it," Josh maintained.

"So what are you suggesting?"

"That we *both* go around the island showing people a picture of Roger. Together. That way, if a situation gets sticky, I'll be right there to rescue you."

"You make me sound like some kind of damsel in distress," she objected. "I've been taking care of myself for a long time now."

"So you've already told me. But everybody needs some help now and again. Especially when you approach a guy in a bar and tell him you're looking for a man."

His reference to the recent incident reminded her of a question she'd been meaning to ask him. "How did you know where I was tonight?"

"I followed you," Josh readily admitted. "I had a feeling you were going to get into trouble again. And I was right."

"It must be nice, always being right," she said in a saccharine voice.

"Don't go getting on your high horse," he

reprimanded her. "If we're going to find Bass, we'll have to do it as a team." That idea fit in with Josh's plan of seduction perfectly. Spending time with Pam would not only make sure she stayed out of trouble, it would also ensure that she stayed at his side. His blue eyes gleamed with anticipation at the thought.

Pam, however, was already having second thoughts about the whole thing. She doubted if Josh really knew the meaning of the word *teamwork*. He wasn't the kind of man to consult with anyone else before making decisions. And if he played leader, that meant Pam would be expected to play follower, a role she avoided like the plague. No, the more she thought about it, the more she was convinced that it wasn't a good idea for her and Josh to become a team.

In an attempt to convince him, she said, "I'm here on business, but this is supposed to be a vacation for you. You don't want to waste your time chasing down Roger."

Actually Josh thought the chances of ever finding Roger were slim to impossible. The guy had probably left the ticket to Bermuda as a red herring to throw Pam off the trail he'd really taken. But that didn't stop Josh from making the most of the situation. "Nonsense. Two heads are better than one. I'm sure that together the two of us can come up with something."

Pam was afraid that the something they'd come up with would be trouble. But, practically speaking, she had to admit there was some advantage to having Josh assist her.

"I don't know. I'll have to think about it," she said.

"You do that." Josh smiled at her and ran a caressing finger down her cheek. "It's been a long day. Why don't you go to bed and get some rest. We'll regroup at breakfast in the morning."

After Josh had left, the memories remained. Pam went to bed, but she couldn't sleep. Instead she stared at the ceiling and brooded about the way she'd responded to Josh. Having melted in his arms twice now, Pam couldn't simply dismiss it as a freak occurrence. Her defenses were practically nonfunctional around him, and that worried her.

Granted, Josh was a very sexy man, but she'd kept sexy men at bay before. So how had she ended up in such a quandary now? She should be treating Josh as if he were ragweed and she had severe hay fever. Instead she was actually considering spending time with him.

It was for a good cause, she told herself. As long as she kept her mind on finding Roger and off Josh, she should be safe enough. Not that she was afraid of Josh; fearing him would give him a power she didn't want him to have.

Pam knew it wasn't unusual for a woman to be sexually attracted to a man she knew would be no good for her, but it was unusual for that woman to be Pam. She'd always tried to run her own life and not let it run her. It all seemed to come back to the question of control. No matter how she'd tried to get away from her past, in some ways it followed her still. There was no denying that her experiences as a child had left their mark on her.

At the age of eight she'd already been in the state's Children's Home for a year, after her own parents died in a car accident. Older children took longer to get adopted, she'd been told. She just had to be patient.

Patience had never been her strong suit. Pam had wanted someone to choose her, someone to love her. She'd gotten part of what she wanted. Chuck Warner had chosen her. His wife had gone along with his choice, even though Elise Warner had really wanted to adopt a baby. But Pam hadn't gotten the second part of her wish. She hadn't gotten someone to love her. She'd gotten someone who dominated her.

One of the first things Chuck had done in his role of father was to take his newly expanded family down to the beach. When he'd discovered that Pam had never learned how to swim, he'd immediately picked her up and carried her out into the waters of Lake Michigan.

Pam hadn't been frightened, not at first. She'd trusted blindly, as only children can do. But then, without so much as a word of warning, she'd been dumped abruptly into the chilly water and told to swim. Today's incident had brought back some of the blind panic she'd felt as a child.

The long-ago exercise had ended with Pam being dragged back to shore by her unrepentant adoptive father. She hadn't swum, but she hadn't drowned either. She'd ended up taking lessons at the local community swimming pool, because she was determined never to be completely dependent on someone else again, at least not in the water. That determination had driven her to win the swimming medals she'd told Josh about.

As Pam got older, things had only gotten worse. She hadn't been physically neglected, but her adoptive father had done everything he could to crush her spirit. He hadn't succeeded. She'd gotten out as soon as she could, with her sanity and her freedom. Ever since then she'd had an aversion to being told what to do.

Thinking about the past gave Pam night-mares that night, and she woke up the next morning with the uneasy image in her mind of a man with sun-bleached hair and wicked blue eyes riding to her rescue. A shower helped clear her mind. Her number-one priority was finding Roger, and if Josh could help her in that, then so be it.

Since she figured that she'd be on the go most of the day, she put on a peach-color terry knit jumpsuit. The fact that the outfit was very flattering played no part in her decision, or so she told herself as she got off the elevator and headed for the resort's airy café, where breakfast was being served.

Josh was already there, waiting for her. He was sitting at a table overlooking the bay. The floor-to-ceiling windows on three sides gave the alcove the appearance of being perched over the ocean. It didn't surprise her that Josh had managed to get the best table in the place. He was the kind of man who always got what he wanted.

Each time Pam saw Josh, she was disconcerted to find him even more attractive than she remembered. He stood when she approached him, an unexpected courtesy. This morning he was wearing a blue polo shirt that matched his eyes. His jeans looked so faded and snug on his body that they made Pam blush. And she was hardly the blushing type.

"I'm glad you're here," Josh murmured with sexy intimacy. "I'm hungry."

It was hard to think calmly when Josh was looking at her as if she were the only one who could satisfy that hunger. She kept telling herself that Josh's approach was so effective because he'd practiced it so often.

"Keep your mind on food and your hands on the table," she instructed him as he ran a caressing finger down her bare arm while seating her.

"Your elbow is healing nicely," he decided. "Has it been giving you any more pain?"

"No." This unforeseen attraction to Josh was causing her more discomfort than her elbow had done.

Josh didn't give her time to dwell on her thoughts. He handed her a menu and suggested what she should order for breakfast. Pam took great satisfaction in ordering something different.

Josh gave her a look that seemed to say, *Enjoy winning your little battles while you can.*

It was a look that made Pam nervous.

When Josh spoke, she expected some sort of verbal follow-up to the visual seduction he was waging against her. Instead his comment was surprisingly mundane. "You told me you were a travel agent, but you didn't tell me where you and Roger have your agency."

"Chicago."

Josh's look of smug satisfaction made Pam instantly suspicious. "What are you smiling at?" she demanded.

"I've got an office in Chicago," he informed her while buttering a piece of toast.

Pam was surprised. "Chicago? Why? There are no oil fields in Illinois." She didn't like the idea of him having business in Chicago. "I would have thought you'd have your office in Texas or some place like that."

"I do have a smaller satellite office in Texas, but the head office is in Chicago — although I have to admit that I don't actually spend much time there." But he had a suspicion the Windy City was going to hold more interest for him in the future.

"Where do you live?" Pam told herself she was only asking to reassure herself that he didn't actually *live* in Chicago.

"Out of a suitcase most of the time," Josh answered before asking a question of his own. "Have you thought about my offer to help you find Roger?"

"Yes, I've thought about it. And I'm willing to accept your help, providing you understand that I'm the one in charge of the search. Having said that, I'll understand if you want to back out."

"You already know what I want," he replied with a meaningful glance.

"What you want and what you get are two different things," Pam retorted. She looked him straight in the eye. "This is a serious situation for me, Josh. I don't have the time to deal with an insincere offer of help. I have to find Roger, and find him fast. So if you're looking on this exercise as an excuse to get something going between us, you can forget it. That's the last thing I need right now."

Pam's directness was a refreshing change from the women Josh was used to dealing with. She didn't fake anything, and he suspected the same passion and directness would also be reflected in the way she made love. But he knew that until this trouble with her boss was resolved, there was little chance of their relationship moving forward as quickly as he wanted it to.

"My offer is sincere," Josh told her. "I do want you to find Roger. But I want you to promise me one thing: that you won't do anything foolish without checking with me first."

Pam smiled. "You mean after I check with you, then it's okay for me to do something foolish?"

"You know what I mean."

"I know what you mean," she agreed. Unable to resist teasing him as he so often teased her, she reached across the table to lightly pat his cheek, as an indulgent nanny might a recalcitrant ward. "You worry too much. And you shouldn't. It'll give you wrinkles."

It didn't occur to Josh until much later that Pam had successfully avoided making the promise he'd requested.

CHAPTER FIVE

Pam and Josh began the day's search for Roger in Hamilton.

"It's the largest city in Bermuda; it makes sense to start there," Josh had told her.

Pam hadn't agreed. "I've already been to Hamilton."

"You were only in the nightclubs. And the visit to Doc's office doesn't count."

"I'm not here to see the sights," she reminded him.

"I know that. But Roger may be seeing the sights, in which case we'll see Roger."

Since renting another moped had been out of the question and taking taxis all the time was too hard on Pam's budget, they'd taken a bus. After reaching Hamilton, they headed for the crowded length of Front Street, where tourists were busy sightseeing and shopping. The buildings were painted in various pastel colors and trimmed with white, as were most of the homes and businesses on the island. Pam saw signs of Bermuda's close ties to Britain all around her. A policeman, wearing bermuda shorts and the shirt and helmet of a British bobbie, was directing traffic from a birdcagelike structure in the center of the intersection.

Pam and Josh visited every store along Front Street. While Josh showed Roger's photo to the various sales personnel, Pam would check out the shoppers milling around the various displays of international merchandise. There was at least one store for each specialty — Swiss watches, French perfume, Japanese cameras, Irish linen, English china.

Pam resisted the urge to buy everything in sight. But she did give in to the temptation to watch Josh in action. She had to hand it to him, he had a way with people — especially women. The store clerks went out of their way to help him, sometimes providing hazy answers in an attempt to detain him.

"I may have seen him, I can't be sure," one young hopeful was saying in a breathy voice. "Maybe if we talked someplace else I might be able to remember more. I get off at four."

"It sounds like a wonderful idea," Pam heard Josh say. "Unfortunately the lady I'm with is extremely jealous and she's got a violent temper. I'm not afraid for myself, you understand, but for you. She's got a mean right hook."

The salesclerk hurriedly stepped back from the counter she'd been seductively leaning over. "Now that I think about it, I don't recognize the man in your photo. Sorry."

Pam was both amused and irritated at Josh's little charade. What a story! As if she would be jealous of him. And if anyone had reason to fear her temper, it was Josh. He certainly infuriated her more than any man she'd ever met. The problem was, he also attracted her.

As if he were capable of reading her thoughts, Josh turned and waved at her. "There you are, darling," he said, presumably for the salesclerk's benefit.

"That's right," she agreed. "Here I am. The question is: Where's Roger?"

"Come on." Josh took Pam's hand and guided her across the street. Since it was a Saturday and the traffic was busy, Pam welcomed his assistance. She didn't welcome the way he made her feel, however. Her fingers actually tingled!

It wasn't the first time Josh had touched her during the course of their morning. His game plan seemed to be to lull her into a false sense of security by keeping the contact brief and casual at first. Then he started adding extra touches; a provocative caress here, a delicate stroke there.

Josh had just twined his fingers through hers, increasing the intimacy of their hand holding. Actually Pam had never considered the simple act of holding someone's hand to be particularly seductive, but then she'd never experienced the nuances that Josh employed.

Pam was so wrapped up in her thoughts that it took her a moment to realize that Josh had stopped in front of a line of horse-drawn carriages along the wharf area. Pam assumed that Josh was going to ask the drivers if they'd seen Roger, but instead he handed some money over and reserved the first carriage for them.

"What are you doing?" Pam demanded as Josh turned to face her.

Preferring action to words, Josh placed his hands around her waist and lifted her onto the carriage with the fringe on top. Through the material of her jumpsuit Pam could feel the heat of each of his fingers. And that heat remained long after he had released her.

Josh settled beside her with one arm stretched out across the back of the seat, as he'd done the first time she met him when he stashed her in Trevor's cab. He sent her the same devilish grin now as he had done then. His arm didn't stay on the back of the seat for long, however. The first turn they took, Josh's hand came down to curve around her shoulder and his arm tugged her closer to him. Pam didn't know which was louder, the *clip-clop* of the horses' hoofs or the *thump-*

thump of her heart.

"Wouldn't want you falling out," he told her with that telltale gleam in his blue eyes.

"I didn't want to take a carriage ride at all," she retorted.

"Stop glaring at me and keep your eyes on the crowds." His hand cupped her chin as he directed her attention out toward the street. He then ruined her concentration by softly trailing his fingers across her throat.

"This isn't a bad way to cruise around looking for Roger," he murmured in a sexy voice. "It's sure easier on the feet than shopping is."

Pam turned to face him, thereby displacing his hand from its provocative position. She squelched her fluttery nerves and fixed him with a mocking stare. "You mean to tell me that a little bit of shopping is enough to do in a big strong macho man like you?"

His grin was downright wicked as he murmured, "I prefer to expend my energy on more enjoyable pastimes."

"I'm sure you do." Pam didn't need to have a map drawn to know what pastimes he was talking about. "But we're not here for fun; we're here because I have to find Roger."

"So you finally admit it would be fun?"

"I don't admit anything."

"That's okay, Pam. You don't have to

admit anything . . . yet." He surprised her by dropping a brief kiss to her parted lips. "Your kisses have already told me all I need to know."

Unfortunately his kisses had told her *more* than she wanted to know. There was no denying the powerful attraction between them. She felt like a needle being drawn to a magnet, and it wasn't a feeling she relished.

The best way to avoid getting caught in a magnetic field is to keep your distance, which Pam attempted to do for the remainder of the half-hour carriage ride. It was easier said than done. No matter how hard she tried to avoid it, every time they turned a corner she bumped into Josh, or he bumped into her — she wasn't sure which. But she did know that she was going to be relieved to get out of that carriage.

They finally completed their tour, and as the carriage came to a full stop, the horses abruptly lurched forward, throwing Pam off balance.

"Watch out!" Josh grabbed Pam and tugged her back to safety.

She ended up on his lap, not at all a safe place to be in her book.

For a brief moment she froze. She was aware of the warm denim of his jeans and the even warmer strength of his thighs beneath her. Then she jumped away from him as if she'd been burned.

Josh's restraining arms ensured that she didn't get very far. "Take it easy," he murmured in her ear. "You don't want the horses to stampede, do you?"

Pam didn't know enough about horses to know whether or not they stampeded. She only knew that she couldn't remain perched half-on and half-off Josh's lap.

Pam was eternally grateful to the driver's assistant, who came forward to help her from the carriage. Her beaming smile of appreciation must have been more potent than Josh's glare of disapproval, because the young man stood his ground, holding out his hand and helping her down.

With her feet once again on terra firma, Pam regained her self-control. She was equally determined to maintain her control of the situation. To do otherwise was to court disaster. She was only spending this time with Josh because he was supposed to help her in her search, not distract her from it.

She was disappointed that they hadn't found any sign of Roger in Hamilton, but she wasn't about to give up. "I think our best bet would be to go here" — she pointed to a location on her map of Bermuda — "because it looks like there are a lot of tourist attractions there. Things like the Aquarium, Blue Grotto Dolphin Show, and Crystal Caves."

Pam had no intention of visiting any of the attractions herself, but she hoped to find a restaurant in the area that would have a good view of the passing traffic. That way, if Roger should happen to pass by on his way to any of the numerous sights, she'd have a chance to spot him. Besides, it was lunchtime and she was getting hungry.

The Swizzle Inn served her purpose to a *t*. Inside, the decor was similar to that of an English pub, complete with an energetic game of darts. In order to keep an eye out for Roger, Pam and Josh sat outside.

Pam ordered something called a swizzleburger. Josh ordered the same and added a request for two Bermuda swizzles to drink. He smiled when Pam took her first unsuspecting swallow a few minutes later. Her dark eyes opened wide as the blend of several rums and fruit juices went down oh so smoothly.

"Good, huh?" Josh said.

"Umm . . ."

He leaned across the small table and studied her mouth suggestively. "See, we do agree on something."

Pam's mouth went dry as excitement hummed through her. Josh watched with silent appreciation as she nervously licked her lips. Of course his deliberation only made matters worse, forcing her into taking a healthy swig of her drink.

Who would have thought the day would ever come when you'd be reduced to mush by a mere look? Pam asked herself in exasperation. *Get a hold of yourself before he gets a hold of you!*

Luckily their waiter arrived with their swizzleburgers at that moment, again saving Pam from Josh's web of seduction.

Chastising herself for getting waylaid by personal issues, Pam determinedly returned her attention to finding Roger. But despite her good intentions, her mind kept wandering back to Josh. It was hard not to when their knees kept bumping under the tiny table.

Pam noted the way Josh relished his food and unthinkingly commented on it. "You've got quite an appetite."

"So I've been told," he murmured with mocking humor.

You walked right into that one. "Where do you think we should go from here? And no erotic answers, please."

Josh gave her a "who me?" look before replying. "Castle Harbor seems like the next best bet. There's a large resort over there."

Josh wasn't kidding when he said it was large. A pamphlet they picked up inside the lobby stated that there were 250 acres of landscaped grounds, and Pam had no reason to doubt that claim.

Again they checked with the reception desk and various other resort personnel, showing them Roger's picture and asking if anyone had seen him. Again they came up with nothing.

Pam couldn't help it. She was getting discouraged. Feeling the need for a little privacy, Pam excused herself and headed for the ladies' room.

She was standing in front of a mirror reapplying her lipstick when she heard a woman ask, "Excuse me, does this belong to you?"

Pam turned to find a young woman holding Roger's photo, which must have fallen out of her purse when she'd taken out her lipstick. She was about to take it when the woman suddenly frowned and studied the photo more carefully.

"Hey, you know Billy too?" the woman exclaimed.

"You know the man in this picture?" Pam asked, unable to believe her luck.

"Yeah, I know him. Well, I've met him, anyway. His name is Billy, but you must know that already."

"Sure," Pam fibbed, "but I don't know where he's staying. You see, he's a friend of mine and I haven't been able to get in touch with him since I've come to Bermuda. I lost the phone number he gave me."

"I know how that can be," the other woman said agreeably. "I'm always losing things. I'm sorry that I don't know Billy's phone number, but I do know that he's going to be at Victor's party tonight. You'll be able to see him there."

When Pam left the ladies' room a short while later, her optimism was restored. Finally she'd gotten a lead! Better than that, she'd gotten the name of the private country club where Roger/Billy was supposed to show up tonight. Now her next problem was how to get into that party.

"What took you so long?" Josh demanded when she returned. "I thought you'd fallen in."

"You worry too much."

"Only about you. And I've got good cause," he added wryly.

"Remember, you're not going to mention mopeds or drowning," she reminded him with a disapproving glare.

"How about stampeding horses?" he countered.

"Hey, that carriage ride was your idea. I would have been fine on my own."

"Mmm, I've heard that before."

"Then pay attention to it."

"Oh, I intend to pay attention to you, Pam. Lots of attention."

That's what she was afraid of! "Let's concentrate on finding Roger, shall we?"

"Maybe it would help if you told me a little more about your boss," Josh suggested. "Does he have any hobbies? Any interests that might give us an idea of where to look for him?"

"I don't know about any hobbies, but he does like plants."

"Great. Then we'll stop at the Botanical Gardens."

What could she say? Don't bother, I got a lead in the ladies' room? She didn't want Josh to know about that or he'd follow her to the party, so she went along with him to the Botanical Gardens.

The carefully tended gardens contained every plant indigenous to Bermuda as well as thousands specially imported for the collection. Beautiful though the display was, Pam was not impressed by the surrounding flora and fauna.

"I don't see any sign of Roger here," she announced within five minutes of their arrival. "Too bad. We'd better start heading back; it's getting late."

Josh sent her a perplexed look. "Is something wrong?" Raising a hand, he brushed her cheek with the back of his fingers. "You look flushed."

Pam skittered away from him. "Must be sunburn."

"The sun isn't shining."

"It was earlier," she said. "But you're right. Now that you mention the weather, it looks like it's going to rain. We'd better leave before it does."

No sooner had she said that than the first heavy drops started falling. Thunder growled in the distance as they ran for the cover of a banyan tree. By the time they reached it they were both soaked.

"See? I told you we should have left," Pam griped. Her terry jumpsuit may have soaked up the water like a thirsty towel, but her hair hadn't fared as well. Wet, it was curlier than usual, and even wilder-looking. The dark strands trickled water down her face and neck. "Now look at us!"

Josh was already looking at her. "Rainwater looks good on you," he told her with a grin. He leaned closer to lick a droplet of rain from her forehead. "Tastes good, too."

Pam's heart was beating so hard she couldn't hear herself think. Not that she was capable of forming any clear thoughts at that moment anyway. Josh had only to touch her and she quivered. No one had ever done that to her before.

His eyes darkened as he stared at her. She

couldn't look away. He made her feel wild and reckless. Spellbound, she watched him reach out to slowly smooth a wet tendril of hair away from her face. His hand lingered to trace her features one by one — her eyes, her nose, and finally her mouth.

He didn't speak. He didn't have to. She knew he wanted to kiss her. Her lips parted, and her breathing became ragged. He tipped up her chin and lowered his mouth to hers. Keeping his eyes open, he kissed her — a light, teasing kiss that made her want more.

"That's enough." Pam's voice was distressingly unsteady.

"Is it?" he questioned huskily. "Not for me. And not for you either." He slid his fingers to the inside of her wrist and felt her pulse. "Your heart's racing almost as much as mine is." He took her hand in his and drew it to his chest. "Feel it?"

The heat of his body spread from her fingertips right up her arm. She was tempted to fling herself into his arms, but she resisted. Lifting a mocking eyebrow, she gave him a look that she hoped was dismissive. "So we're back to playing touchy-feely again, are we?"

Josh lifted her hand to his mouth so he could kiss her palm. "But we do it so well."

I know, she thought to herself as she snatched

her hand away. *That's what worries me.*

"Look, the rain's over," she said, hoping to distract him. "Since you do everything so well, how about finding us a taxi?"

Of course Josh was able to hail a cab with no difficulty at all. As fate would have it, Trevor was once again driving the cab.

"How nice to see you two together again," Trevor said. "Where would you like to go?"

To bed, was the answer Pam saw written in Josh's wicked blue eyes.

Forget it, she replied in kind.

Pam never stopped to consider how unusual it was to converse so clearly without speaking a single word. She simply narrowed her own gaze and glared at Josh.

"Are you enjoying your stay here in Bermuda?" Trevor asked them.

"Immensely," Josh replied, while the intimate direction of his eyes told Pam exactly what it was he *really* enjoyed immensely.

Pam didn't trust herself to say a word as Trevor directed another question at Josh. "You were touring the sites today?"

"Sure was." Josh's devilish eyes were leisurely touring Pam's body.

"And what did you see?" Trevor inquired.

"Not as much as I'd like to."

"You've seen as much as you're going to!" Pam hissed in a furious whisper.

"Don't make promises you can't keep," Josh countered.

Pam tried not to let him get to her. She had to concentrate on getting into that private party tonight. So when Josh later brought up the subject of dinner, she told him, "I'm having dinner in my room."

"Sounds good to me."

"Alone."

"Sounds lonely to me."

"It sounds good to me. It's been a long day."

"You seem in an awful hurry to get rid of me," Josh complained as he helped her out of the cab. "I wonder why that is?"

"I don't know what you mean." Pam headed for the elevators.

Josh followed her. "I think you do. And I think I know why you're acting this way."

Her hand froze on the call button. "You do?"

"I think it's got something to do with what happened between us at the Botanical Gardens."

"Nothing happened between us," Pam denied.

"Not yet, but it will." His voice was low and seductive. "You can run for the time being, but you're not going to be able to hide for much longer."

She knew her time was running out in more ways than one. When she was in Josh's arms she forgot everything else — and that was dangerous.

Pam now had an additional motivation for finding Roger as soon as possible — so she could get away from Josh before she got in over her head. If things went as she hoped, she should be able to grab Roger and head back to Chicago first thing in the morning.

It wasn't until she was standing in front of the private club later that evening that Pam realized the difficulty of getting inside. The club was located near the exclusive enclave of Tucker's Town, a retreat for millionaires, and it obviously catered to the same elite clientele.

"Can I help you, ma'am?" she was courteously but coolly asked by a liveried doorman.

"Yes, I'm here for Victor's party."

Pam prayed he wouldn't ask her "Victor who?" because she didn't know her supposed host's surname. Luck seemed to be with her, because the man's question turned out to be "What's your name?" He pulled out what appeared to be a guest list attached to a clipboard.

"Ms. Smith." Pam figured there had to be at least one Smith on the list.

She was wrong. "I'm sorry, but I don't see your name here."

"Are you sure?" Pam tried moving closer and getting a look at the list herself, but the doorman wouldn't have any of it. He held the clipboard very close to his gold-buttoned vest. "Did you check both spellings?"

"Yes. Nothing even close to Smith."

Pam gave him an appealing look. "Ah, maybe it's under my maiden name. Jones?"

The doorman shook his head.

A minor setback, Pam told herself as the doorman was distracted by more arrivals. She had to consider her options and do it quickly. Considering the fact that two more liveried men stood on either side of the entrance, she figured her chances of slipping inside with the rest of the crowd were not very good. The best she could hope for would be to conceal herself and wait for Roger to arrive. A bank of ornamental shrubbery flanking the entryway looked like a good bet.

She checked to make sure no one was looking before making her move. With seeming nonchalance she walked over to one of the flowering bushes and pretended to inhale its heady scent. A second later she'd stepped behind it and swiftly dropped into a crouch. Unfortunately the thick underbrush snagged both her black silk pants and matching chemise top. The ground was still damp from the rain earlier in the day, so she couldn't sit or kneel to make herself more comfortable. Her knees began to ache as group after group of people went by, but there was still no sign of Roger.

Pam had no premonition of trouble. Aside from the fact that her right leg was falling asleep, there were no other signs of impending danger. One minute she was peeking between the bushes, and the next she was abruptly muzzled and being dragged backward into the darkness — away from any possibility of help.

CHAPTER SIX

Pam fought back. She kicked and scratched. It didn't help. Seconds later she was hauled behind a thick tree trunk and forcibly shaken.

"Stop it, you idiot!"

Recognizing Josh's voice, Pam stopped struggling and squinted in the darkness, trying to make out his face. He'd changed, and not just his clothes. Along with the black jeans and T-shirt, he wore an expression of savage fury. His eyes no longer gleamed with mockery; they burned with anger.

Pam wasn't exactly thrilled herself. How dare he treat her like this, scaring her half to death! His hand was still across her mouth so her words were completely muffled, which was just as well. Their content was definitely not ladylike.

"You keep that up and we'll both be arrested for trespassing," he coolly informed her.

The idea of Josh being jailed was very appealing, but Pam had no desire to join him there. So she kept silent.

"That's better. Come on, we've got to get out of here before we're caught. The grounds are filled with security guards." Josh didn't give her a chance to reply. He simply tossed her over his shoulder in a fireman's lift and carried her.

Pam would have protested, but his move knocked the air right out of her. As she hung upside down, her first wild thought was relief that she hadn't eaten dinner! Her second thought was to free herself, but her squirming only made things worse. Pam's head was reeling by the time they reached the taxi, but she soon regained both her equilibrium and the use of her voice after she'd been bundled inside.

Josh raised an eyebrow at some of the curses she was using but otherwise showed no sign of being upset by her obvious anger.

"Are you crazy?" she lashed out indignantly. "Who do you think you are, sneaking up on me like that — let alone dragging me away and then tossing me over your shoulder like some bag of potatoes!"

"I should have guessed what you were up to earlier," Josh said in a harsh voice. "But I mistakenly believed that you'd honor your promise."

"I never promised you anything!"

"We had an agreement!" He rapped out the words. "I helped you on the condition that you talk to me before pulling any more stunts.

You knew that, and you pretended to go along with it."

"I never asked you for your help," she reminded him. "Now thanks to the stunt you just pulled, I missed my chance of finding Roger, and it's all your fault!"

"What are you talking about?"

Pam gave him a look that could have burned a hole through steel. "Why do you think I was hiding in those bushes? For my own amusement? I found someone who recognized Roger, only she called him Billy. He was supposed to show up tonight for some party. I wasn't able to get into the club, so I was waiting outside for him."

"You were trespassing on private property. What did you think would happen if you were found? Did you think they'd just slap your wrist and send you home?"

"I never thought I'd be attacked by someone I thought I knew," she retorted.

"You didn't think, period. You never do."

"Oh, so now you're an expert on my behavior, is that it?"

"If I hadn't been the one to find you, you could have gotten into serious trouble tonight."

"You did find me, and I still got into serious trouble!" Pam sent him a resentful look and rubbed her sore arms. "I doubt if the security guards would have treated me as badly as you did."

Josh was not at all remorseful. "You deserved it. Somebody's got to make you realize the consequences of your rash actions."

Josh and Pam were so wrapped up in their argument that they didn't even realize the cab had reached their hotel until the driver turned to inform them of that fact.

Josh immediately clamped a hand around Pam's wrist, thereby preventing her fast getaway.

She was livid. "Let go of me!"

"We're not done talking yet." He marched her over to the elevators.

"We haven't been talking at all." She yanked her elbow from his grasp. "We've been yelling!"

"Because that appears to be the only way to stop you from acting like an idiot," he retorted.

Josh kept her so busy refuting his angry accusations about her mental competency that she wasn't able to get into her room and slam the door in his face as she'd planned. She tried, but he simply shoved the door open again with the palm of his hand and stormed inside right after her.

"We've played this scene before," Pam stated with icy fury. "I have no interest in doing it again. Get out of my room!"

"You still don't realize the seriousness of your actions, do you?" His voice was grim. "You still think you're playing some sort of treasure hunt with Roger as the grand prize. Well, let me tell you, honey, you got in over your head tonight. You could have ended up in jail — did you ever stop to consider that? The authorities here take trespassing very seriously. And that country club is one of the most exclusive in the world. If you'd been caught, they would have pressed criminal charges against you."

"All right, already. I get the idea," she muttered. Her face was pale, her expression bleak.

"I hope you do." Josh had no regrets about scaring her, if that was what it took to stop her from acting so rashly again. The possibility of her being harmed was something he'd do anything to prevent.

"Now what are you doing?" she demanded as Josh picked up her phone and began dialing an outside number.

"I'm going to find out if anyone named Billy ever showed at that party. Who did you say was giving it?"

"His name is Victor. That's all I know."

Pam sat on the bed and kicked off her muddy shoes while Josh tried to charm information out of whoever was on the other end of the phone. "That's right, his name is Billy. In his early fifties, reddish hair, medium height, a little on the heavy side. Yes, I'll hold." Josh sat down next to Pam. "He's already left? How long ago? I see. Any idea how I can get in touch with him? Well, thanks anyway."

"He *was* there!" Pam exclaimed, jumping to her feet. "I told you he would be." She paced back and forth, angrily muttering all the while. "I would have been able to talk to him if you hadn't interfered. This whole thing could have been over with by now."

"That's right. If you'd told me what you were up to, I could have helped you get in to speak to Roger. But no, you had to try and do things your own way."

"Instead of doing things your way, huh?"

"Instead of doing it the right way."

Pam stopped her pacing to glare at him. "As far as you're concerned, your way is the only right way of doing anything. You don't even know the meaning of the word *teamwork*," she accused him.

"You're not exactly a pro at it either. Instead of sharing your information with me, you went off half-cocked on your own."

Pam's eyes narrowed. "I don't have to share anything with you. Besides, I knew you'd disapprove of my plan and I was right."

"It was a stupid plan and it almost got you into a great deal of trouble. And don't you dare tell me you could have handled it, or I'll —"

"Or you'll what?" she asked. "Manhandle me the way you did in those bushes? Knock some sense into me?"

"I'd like to, believe me."

"You do and you'll be walking funny for a week!"

"Would you get it through that thick skull of yours that I care about you!" he yelled.

Pam was speechless. That was the last thing she had expected him to say.

"Oh, what the hell. Come here." He tugged her onto the bed and rolled over, pinning her down on the mattress.

"Josh!" Touching as they were from shoulder to thigh, she was very much aware of his masculinity.

"I'm tired of arguing with you," he muttered. The raw intensity of his look made her shiver.

Pam's hair was spread out like a dark sea around her face. Unable to wait a moment longer, Josh buried his hands in the silky mass and lowered his mouth to hers. He kissed her fiercely, making no effort to disguise his hunger. Pam felt as if she were burning up from the inside out. This swift transition from anger to passion was very exciting. She drank in his potent kisses, becoming addicted to their taste. When the thrust of his tongue became intensely evocative, Pam responded with sexy moves of her own.

His murmurs of approval were incorporated into their kisses. Pam's reasons for avoiding Josh were forgotten, wiped out by her need for him. Now that the embrace was no longer one-sided, Josh allowed his fingers to move from her hair down to her throat.

Pam responded by sliding her arms around his waist and tugging him even closer. His knee nudged its way between hers, making her very much aware of his arousal. The thin silk of her clothing slid seductively against his jeans, causing such a pleasurable friction that she moved against him again and again.

She could only express herself with throaty moans and soft sighs. The uneven pounding of her heart was matched by the erratic beat of his as Josh's kisses strayed from her lips to the sensitive hollow behind her ear. Her skin tingled wherever his warm mouth brushed it.

"Feel what you do to me," he growled, taking her hand and guiding it to his chest.

Pam opened her eyes so that she could not only feel but also see what she did to him. She saw the need reflected in his smoky eyes, in the etched tautness of his features. She knew she should stop, but the hands that were meant to push him away disobeyed orders and instead stole around his neck to pull him closer.

He felt so good against her, so right. Tugging his T-shirt from the waistband of his jeans, she slid her hands beneath the material to caress his back. He was warm and strong, and he shuddered when she raked her nails across his bare skin. Her eyes glowed with the knowledge that she excited him, and she became even bolder in her explorations.

"You're driving me crazy," he muttered.

Twining one hand in her hair, Josh tugged her head back and fiercely kissed the soft line of her throat while his other hand moved down her body from her shoulder to her hip and back again. Then his attention shifted to her silk chemise as he hooked his fingers beneath the spaghetti straps and oh so slowly smoothed them down her arms. Seconds later her chemise was gone.

Pam shivered as a sudden draft of air-conditioned air assailed her bare skin. Her chill soon turned to feverish heat as Josh warmed her with his hands, treating her to ardent strokes from his skillful fingers before covering her breasts with his palms.

"Still cold?" he asked in a husky whisper.

Pam shook her head. She wasn't capable of

speech. His caresses had her breathless. But Josh wasn't content to merely seduce her with his touch. He devoured her with his eyes and wooed her with his words.

"You're so beautiful. So golden. Look how perfectly you fit into the palm of my hand. And you feel as good as you look. Soft, like satin. Warm satin. I wonder if you taste as good as you feel."

Lowering his head, he opened his mouth and tasted her breast. Wild excitement coursed through Pam, making her arch against him. Josh took pleasure in her unmistakable signs of arousal and continued to work his magic on her. A warm nibble was followed by the ravishing swirl of his tongue. As the intimacy of his caresses increased, so, too, did the pleasure.

Unable to stand the delicious torment a second longer, Pam twisted hungrily beneath him. An aching need for completion was building within her, blinding her to the danger of her actions. She couldn't resist him or what he was doing to her.

When Josh reached for the side fastening of her silk pants, bells went off. It took her a second to realize that the sound wasn't imagined but was actually the phone ringing. The sudden interruption was like a gust of wind dispersing the clouds of passion.

"Ignore it," Josh muttered.

But Pam couldn't do that. She reached for the phone as if grabbing for a lifeline.

"Hello?"

"Pam, it's Anita. You were supposed to call me. What happened? Is everything all right?"

It was hard for Pam to answer when Josh was running his fingers down her bare back. She glared at him but it made no difference. He just grinned and refused to hand her the robe she was pointing at.

"Uh, hold on a second, Anita. There's someone at the door." Pam put the phone down, grabbed the robe and belted it before turning to do battle with Josh.

"There's no one at the door," he said. He lay sprawled on her bed, looking perfectly at home. Actually, with his tousled hair and roguish smile, he looked perfect.

"You've got to get out of here."

Josh seemed amused by her urgency. "Now why would I want to do that?"

"Because you don't want to push your luck."

"Luck has nothing to do with it," Josh murmured.

"Careful," she tartly advised. "Your ego is showing." Sighing, she decided to tell the truth. "Look, Josh, I'm really not ready to deal with this now."

"How do I know that if I leave, you won't go and pull some other silly stunt?"

"Because I've got no desire to be tossed over your shoulder and dragged back here again."

"Maybe not, but you do have other desires, don't you, Pam?"

"Yes." She tugged him off the bed. "And right now my main desire is getting you out of my room!"

"What's wrong?" he asked mockingly as she steered him toward the door. "Afraid you might be getting in over your head?"

"I'm not afraid of you, just distrustful of your motives," Pam said while opening the door.

"What's to be distrustful about?" He paused to trail a finger down her throat. "I assure you, my motives are purely . . . improper."

"I know it."

"And you liked it."

"Good night, Josh." Pam closed the door with a decided slam.

Out in the hallway Josh was smiling to himself as he murmured, "She's wild about me."

Inside her room, a flustered Pam was speaking to Anita.

"Did I interrupt something?" Anita asked.

"No!" Pam drew in a deep breath and spoke in a more normal tone of voice. "I'm sorry I didn't call earlier, but I got a lead. I finally found someone who'd seen Roger. He was supposed to show up at some sort of party tonight. Unfortunately I wasn't allowed into the party."

"Was Roger there?"

"Apparently so," Pam replied.

"That's something, I suppose. At least we know he's still in Bermuda. Where do you think he could be hiding out?"

"I don't know, but I plan on finding out."

Surprisingly, Pam's next lead came from Josh. Over breakfast the next morning he casually mentioned that the person he'd spoken to on the phone last night had suggested looking for Roger/Billy in St. George.

"Why didn't you tell me this last night?" Pam demanded.

"I was distracted," Josh replied with a meaningful look. "Besides, I figured you'd probably take off on your own if I told you then."

"Is there anything else you're hiding from me?"

"Lots. Wanna see it all?"

Pam laughed at Josh's leer. "Thanks anyway, but I think I'll pass."

"You don't know what you're missing."

"Yes, I do." Pam's memory was very vivid,

and the swimsuit she'd seen him in had left little to the imagination. Having caressed his body, Pam knew that he felt even better than he looked.

"Such willpower," Josh marveled.

Pam rolled her eyes and rose to her feet. "I don't know about you, but I'm going to St. George."

"Not without me you're not."

Pam was still telling Josh he was impossible when they arrived in the town of St. George.

A sizable crowd had gathered in the King's Square to watch a show being presented for the passengers of the cruise ship that was docked nearby. A costumed town crier, complete with tricornered hat and buckled shoes, was circling the square and ringing a large brass bell to get everyone's attention. "Hear ye, hear ye!" he cried.

"Let's go see what's going on," Josh said.

The show began with a young man being led to a platform.

"What are they doing?" Pam asked.

Her question was answered by the town crier, who announced that this disgraceful sailor was being put in the stocks for being a drunk and making a public nuisance of himself.

"You see what happens to rogues." Pam gave Josh a considering look. "I'll bet you were a pirate in another lifetime." An eye patch might diminish the powerful effect of his blue eyes, but it would add a rakish edge to his already good looks. Now that she'd spent more time with Josh, she knew that his self-assurance was as much a part of him as his running shoes. Being a rogue came naturally to him.

"You really think I look like a pirate?" Josh looked pleased at the idea.

"You act like one, too — tossing me over your shoulder last night."

"Ah, but I made it up to you later, didn't I?" He watched her face. "What's that? A blush?"

"No way. I never blush."

"There's a first time for everything, Pam."

She was saved from replying by a round of applause and laughter from the crowd as several other costumed players threw orange peels at the erring man. The show then moved on to the dunking chair.

As the crowd shifted from one side of the square to the other, Pam looked for Roger. She couldn't help noticing how many men, young and old, were wearing shorts. None of them looked as good as Josh did in his white tennis shorts and blue polo shirt. And none of them resembled Roger.

After she and Josh had toured the sights,

they started checking the stores.

"An entire store just for perfume?" Josh said.

Pam gave the place a quick look around. "Roger's not in here."

"Wait — while we're here we might as well check things out." Josh took her by the hand and led her over to the counter. "Here, try this one." Removing a glass stopper from a shapely bottle, he dabbed her wrist with scent. Then he made a big production out of lifting her arm so that he could sniff the perfume and judge its effectiveness for himself.

"Forbidden Nights. No, I've had too many of those lately already. Let's try another one. Ah, this sounds more promising: Seduction." He repeated the sampling procedure on her other wrist, this time dabbing perfume all the way up her arm. "Nice, very nice." Josh brushed his lips across her skin as he spoke.

Nice was putting it mildly, Pam thought to herself. Actually *naughty* came much closer to the way she was feeling right now.

"Why don't you go check out the shop next door," Pam suggested in an uneven voice.

"Because I'm having too much fun right here," he answered.

His tongue darted out to mark his place, indicating the "right here" he was talking about.

"Stop that!" Pam tugged her arm away from him.

Josh released her, but he continued making such outrageous comments that she ended up practically kicking him out of the perfume shop.

Since Josh wanted to buy her something he'd seen in a store around the corner, he agreed. "I'll meet you back here in twenty minutes."

Pam had just finished purchasing a bottle of Seduction perfume when she caught sight of a man with red hair. Grabbing her package, she hurried out of the store. For a second she thought she'd lost him, but then the crowd on the sidewalk parted and she saw him again. He was too far away for her to be certain it was Roger, but it certainly looked like him from the back.

Pam trailed the man, hoping to get a better look at him. But he didn't turn around. Instead he headed directly for the huge cruise ship and boarded it. Pam paused for a moment and then followed him. She was stopped at the entryway by a Bermuda port official who wanted to see her passenger identification.

Pam dug through her purse and flashed a brilliant smile at one of the ship's officers who stood nearby. "I know it's in here someplace."

Meanwhile the line of passengers behind her started complaining.

"Go on in," the official said.

"Thanks."

Once inside, Pam found no sign of the man who could be Roger. Playing the part of a passenger, she asked the purser if Roger was listed on the passenger manifest. He wasn't. But the purser thought Roger's photo looked familiar. He suggested checking with the ship's photographer, who suggested checking with someone else.

Busy following the chain of leads, Pam didn't realize how much time had passed since she'd boarded the ship. She was questioning the bartender in the observation lounge when she suddenly realized that the scenery outside the picture windows was no longer stationary.

"This ship is moving!" she exclaimed.

"That's right, ma'am. We're underway."

Dismayed, Pam dropped onto a bar stool. "Great," she muttered. "We're underway, and I'm in big trouble."

CHAPTER SEVEN

Josh was furious. Where could Pam have gone? St. George was only a small town; how the hell could he have lost her so quickly?

He'd returned to the perfume store in ten minutes, not twenty, and still he'd missed her. She must have left as soon as she'd gotten rid of him. God only knew what kind of trouble she'd managed to get herself into by now.

Shoving an impatient hand through his hair, Josh cursed softly. He'd never had such trouble with a woman before. Pam was driving him crazy. The more he saw of her, the more he wanted her — and the more he worried about her. He never knew what stunt she'd pull next. That uncertainty, added to his passion for her, had resulted in sleepless nights and cold showers.

Vowing that she was going to make up every restless minute to him, Josh checked his watch again. She'd been missing for two hours now, and he'd questioned just about everyone he could find. Since the cruise ship had weighed anchor and left, the town was no longer crowded and he was running out of options.

"Excuse me," a uniformed customs official said. "Are you the man who was inquiring about your missing companion?" When Josh nodded, the man went on to ask, "This woman you're looking for, does she have dark hair?"

"Yes. She's in her late twenties, about so high." Josh held his hand to a point just beneath his chin.

"Well, I did let a woman board who didn't show me her passenger identification, and it sounds like she might fit your description."

"She boarded the cruise ship?" Josh questioned in disbelief.

"That's right. She was a passenger, wasn't she?"

Josh didn't even hear the man's question. "Where's that ship going?"

"It will dock in Hamilton tomorrow morning. Why? Is there something wrong, sir?" the official questioned.

"Nothing I can't take care of," Josh answered. His blue eyes narrowed decisively. This had been going on long enough. It was time he took matters into his own hands.

Meanwhile, out at sea, Pam was morosely staring at the glass of ice water she'd been nursing for the past hour. She would have ordered a drink, but the ship's bartender had told her that he couldn't accept cash; the drink had to be charged to her stateroom. Since she didn't have a stateroom, she didn't have a drink. Discouraged, Pam wondered how she had ended up in this situation.

She could well imagine Josh's reaction to her disappearance. He'd been mad at her before, but she had a feeling he was really going to hit the roof over this one. She could hear him now. "I let you out of my sight for ten minutes and you get into trouble!" Had she been born under an unlucky star or what? she wondered glumly.

Normally Pam wouldn't have indulged in the brief bout of self-pity, but she was tired. She was tired of searching for Roger, tired of following dead-end leads. She was a travel agent, not a private detective!

She was also tired of fighting her feelings for Josh. When she'd first run into him, she'd been so sure she knew what kind of man he was. But now that she'd spent more time with him, she saw another side of him that she found almost irresistible. She knew he was cocky and self-assured, experienced in the seduction of women. But he was also warm and caring, and sexy as all get-out.

The day had started off so well. She and Josh had actually been working as a team. They hadn't even argued all day, and she'd enjoyed being with him. It had been nice having someone share this responsibility she'd been saddled with. It had been nice sharing other things with Josh as well. Like that kiss last night.

Her gaze became dreamy as the memories returned. Josh had a way of making the slightest touch memorable. The feel of his fingers threading through hers was as exciting as any embrace she'd ever known. With that kind of potential, she could only imagine what making love with him would be like! His kisses already set her on fire. Lying next to him, touching him, sharing the most erotic intimacies. . . . Just thinking about it aroused her.

Pam left the observation lounge in an embarrassed hurry. Perhaps it would be best if she kept her mind on business for the time being. Taking a walk around the ship, she kept her eyes peeled for Roger, or his red-haired look-alike. It was ironic that she should end up marooned on a cruise ship. The money Roger had stolen was from clients who had booked passage on a cruise.

Pam had been the one who'd recommended the trip. She'd been on several cruises before, quickie trips down to the Caribbean geared for travel agents. But this ship was much larger than those had been. This one had eleven decks and two swimming pools, and the thing felt like it was twice the length of Manhattan. A stroll along the promenade deck turned out to be a major hike. She'd lost count of how many public rooms she'd walked through, each one more luxurious than the last.

As the hour grew later, Pam became more and more conscious of not having a stateroom. A late-night buffet had been set up on the upper deck, so at least she didn't go hungry. Pam, who hadn't eaten since breakfast, grabbed a plate and piled it high with fresh fruit, cold cuts, cheese and crackers. She thought she'd escaped attention, but she was soon spotted by a man who fancied himself a smooth talker.

"You seem lonely, little lady. Mind if I join you?"

Her eyes narrowed dangerously. "Yes, I do mind."

As the man beat a hasty retreat, Pam sat in a deck chair and wondered why the same come-on from Josh would have made her heart beat faster. What was it about him that got to her? She'd seen several men on the ship tonight who were good-looking, but they'd all left her cold.

She couldn't ignore the facts any longer. Josh was right. She did want him. Why couldn't they have met under other circumstances, when she had the time and peace of mind to get involved?

Involved? she repeated to herself in dismay. What was she thinking of? Josh didn't want to get involved with her, he wanted to make love with her. The two were not synonymous. He certainly hadn't given her any indication that he looked on this as anything other than a holiday fling. The problem was that for the first time in her life, Pam wouldn't have minded having a holiday fling — if only everything else wasn't in such a mess.

It was a long night. By the next morning Pam was in a rotten mood. Her eyes were gritty, and her head was swimming. At first she was relieved to see Josh waiting for her when she disembarked. For one moment she was even tempted to throw herself into his arms. But then she saw the anger in Josh's eyes and her mood worsened.

"Have a nice trip?" he asked pleasantly.

"Don't start with me!" she warned him. "I've had a rough night."

"Serves you right," Josh retorted. "You're lucky that ship wasn't headed out to sea. If it had, your next port of call could have been Borneo!"

Pam swallowed back the threat of tears. "I wasn't planning on stowing away. I didn't know the damn boat would move as soon as I got on it!"

"It's a ship, not a boat, and you had no business being on it in the first place. Why *did* you get on board?" he asked belatedly.

"I saw someone who looked like Roger," she explained in a flat voice. "I followed him from the perfume store in St. George and saw him get on the ship. I talked my way on board to look for him, but of course I didn't find any sign of him." Pam paused and swayed wearily.

Josh immediately grabbed hold of her. "Look at yourself — you're practically dead on your feet!"

She thought she detected concern in his angry voice, but she was too exhausted to be sure. "I wandered around the damn ship all night . . . afraid that if I sat down . . . I'd fall asleep . . ."

Without waiting for the rest of her explanation, Josh scooped her up into his arms.

Light-headed from lack of sleep, she made no protest. "We've got to stop meeting like this," she murmured against his throat.

"You got part of that right," he muttered while carrying her to a waiting cab. "What's got to stop is this search. Let the police handle it. You've done all you can. Recovering the small change your boss took off with isn't worth the hell you're putting yourself through."

"Small change?" Pam exclaimed as he placed her on the backseat. Turning to face him, she said, "Twenty thousand dollars may be small change to you, but it's a hell of a lot of money to me and to the people who made their deposits! That money represents the dream of a lifetime for seven couples. They saved for years so that they could take a cruise."

"Roger's the one who stole the money, not you."

"You don't understand," she muttered before wearily closing her eyes.

Josh understood only too well. Until Pam got this matter of the missing money settled, they weren't going to get anywhere. Now that he knew exactly how much money was missing, he could set his plan into motion.

Turning to speak to Pam, he realized she was sound asleep. She looked adorable. He hadn't realized how long her lashes were, or how smooth her golden skin was. Her lips were parted, revealing the slight unevenness of her two front teeth. He smiled, imagining her resisting the idea of wearing braces.

When they arrived at the hotel, Josh woke her with a soft kiss.

"Mmmm, nice," she mumbled before burrowing into his shoulder.

"Want me to carry you to your room?"

Pam shook her head but otherwise showed no sign of waking up.

"How about I carry you to *my* room?"

That did get her attention. She sat up abruptly. "I'm awake."

"Sure?"

"Positive."

"Too bad," he murmured wryly. "Come on, then, I'll escort you upstairs." He kept one arm around her as he guided her through the hotel lobby and into the elevator.

Pam told herself she was only leaning against him so she could rest during the short ride to her third-floor room. It took her awhile to find the door key, but when she did, Josh plucked it from her clumsy fingers and opened the door for her.

Following her inside, he suggestively inquired, "Need any more help? Getting out of your clothes, maybe? Or getting into bed?"

Pam kicked off her shoes and gave him a chiding look. "I've been putting myself to bed for some time now. I think I can manage by myself."

"You may manage, but do you enjoy?"

"You know what I'd really enjoy?" she murmured with soft humor.

"No. What?"

"To be left alone so I can get some sleep." She yawned. "I'll see you later, Josh."

"Yes, you will." *Catch up on your sleep while you can, Pam, because you may not get much of it tonight.*

Luckily Pam wasn't looking at him or she would have questioned the satisfied gleam in his blue eyes. As it was, she could hardly keep her own eyes open. The moment she stretched out on the bed she was out like a light.

The next thing she knew the phone was ringing. A groggy look at her travel alarm told her that she'd slept most of the day away!

Trying to sound wide awake, she deliberately made her "Hello" sound alert and perky.

"Pam, it's Anita. Thank God you're all right! I was getting frantic. When you didn't call me yesterday, I tried reaching you last night but there was no answer. What happened?"

Pam flopped back onto the bed with a sigh. "I got stuck on a cruise ship."

"Pam, we must have a bad connection. I thought you said something about a ship."

"I did. There's nothing wrong with the connection. I thought I saw Roger get on board so I followed him. The ship took off before I could *get* off. Luckily it was only cruising around the island and docked in Hamilton this morning, otherwise I might have been calling you from . . . Borneo."

Anita sounded confused. "What was Roger doing on board a cruise ship?"

"I don't know for sure that it was Roger. I couldn't get a clear look at the guy."

"So we're no closer to finding Roger now than we were four days ago?" Anita sounded dismayed. "Pam, what are we going to do? We can't keep this quiet much longer."

"I know that." Pam tried to calm Anita's worries, but it was hard to do when she was so anxious herself. They ended up making a decision that neither welcomed, but both knew it had to be done. "I'll call you in the morning, Anita."

Disheveled and discouraged, Pam took refuge in the shower. The pounding water soothed her taut back muscles but did little to calm her thoughts. An energetic towel-drying of her hair released some nervous frustration. However, one look in the mirror told her that she now looked like a wild woman. Sighing, she ran her fingers through the still-damp strands to coax some semblance of order to the unruly curliness. She couldn't help wishing she could restore order to the rest of her life with equal ease.

Pam was still brooding when Josh knocked on her door.

"What's wrong?" he asked her. "You look

like you've just lost your best friend."

She tightened the belt on her terry-cloth robe and motioned him inside. "I don't know about my best friend, but it looks like I'll be losing my job. I can't keep this from the police any longer. If I don't find Roger by morning, I'm turning the case over to them."

"Is it really Roger you need to find, or just the money?"

"I don't understand."

Josh elaborated. "If you recovered the money, there wouldn't be any real need for you to locate Roger immediately, would there? He may own the travel agency, but from what you've told me, you run it."

"Josh, what are you getting at?"

"I've got some good news and some bad news. Which do you want first?"

"Good news," she answered without hesitation. "It's been so long since I've had any I've almost forgotten what it feels like."

"I met with Roger."

Pam was shocked. "You what? Where is he? Is he coming back? Why didn't you tell me?"

"Calm down. Roger isn't coming back — not for the time being, anyway. But he did give me the money to return to you. He's decided to take a break from the business for a while."

"Wait a minute." Pam held out a hand as if

calling for time out. "I don't get this. You met with Roger and he just handed the money over to you? Why would he do that? He doesn't know you from Adam!"

"He saw us together."

"He did? Where?"

"In Hamilton, not that it really matters. He preferred that I be the one to give the money back to you. He was too upset to face you himself," Josh explained.

"He really gave you the money?"

"Actually it's a cashier's check."

Dazed, she shook her head. "I can't believe this."

"Here it is. See for yourself."

Pain took the check. Her hands shook as she read it. The check for twenty thousand dollars was made out in her name. "He didn't give you any explanation?"

"Just a brief message. Roger wants you to go back to the travel agency and keep the place running like you always have. He'll be in touch."

"Do you know what this means?" Pam exclaimed. "It means that those people can take their cruise! It means that Anita and I won't be out of a job! And it means that Roger won't be arrested!"

"It means we should celebrate," Josh inserted.

"Celebrate? But I should be getting back to Chicago."

"The last flight for Chicago has already left for the day. There's nothing more you can do — not about going home, anyway." There were plenty of other things she could do, though, and he planned on sharing every one of them with her!

Reading Josh's thoughts in his eyes, Pam struggled to remember what she was going to say. "Uh, I've got to call Anita and tell her the good news."

Anita was ecstatic and therefore didn't notice the soft huskiness of Pam's voice. Josh noticed, and was heartened by it. Tonight was theirs.

"Go put on something sexy but practical," he told Pam as soon as she hung up the phone.

"I don't own anything sexy but practical," she said. "The two are exclusive of one another."

"You look sexy in anything you wear. I'm sure you'd look even sexier wearing nothing at all. But that would definitely cause a riot in the lobby, so you'd better put something on." He quickly went through the few things she had hanging in the closet. "How about this?"

"This" turned out to be a thin Indian cotton caftan in muted shades of purple.

Surprisingly Pam wasn't angered by his deciding what she should wear. She was too bemused by his comment about her being sexy. "Are you going to wear something sexy but practical too?"

"Definitely."

"Where are we going?"

"It's a surprise. You'll see. You'll love it, trust me."

"Uh-oh. I don't like the sound of that," she muttered wryly.

"Don't you?" Josh brushed several light kisses from her temple to the corner of her mouth. "How about the feel of this?" His tongue took a teasing swipe across her bottom lip. "You like this, don't you?"

"Too much." Her reply was breathless.

"There's no such thing as too much," he murmured.

"Isn't there?"

"No." He swooped down to capture her mouth with his. Although the kiss only lasted a second or two, it was enough to tempt her — and leave her wanting more.

Releasing her, he stepped away and said, "Get dressed. I'll be back in fifteen minutes."

"Fifteen!" She opened her eyes that were still dreamy with passion. "Wait, I can't be ready that fast —"

But Josh had already left.

Even though Pam took twice her allotted time, Josh didn't complain. His eyes roved over her with blatant appreciation. "It was worth the wait."

"Thank you. You don't look so bad yourself." Sexy and practical did indeed describe the clothes he was wearing. The soft jeans that fit him like a second skin had been teamed with a navy print shirt and a summer-weight beige linen blazer. The faint scent of his aftershave teased her senses.

"Ready?" he asked.

Ready? She was in danger of becoming willing. Gathering her hazy thoughts, Pam tried to remember what she'd meant to say. Something about her outfit, wasn't it?

As if reading her mind, Josh said, "What you're wearing is perfect. We're only going down to the beach."

"The beach!" Somehow that wasn't the answer she'd expected. She'd spent all that time blending eye shadows and putting on perfume just to go to the beach? She'd even applied a new coat of nail polish.

"Stop worrying." Josh smoothed away her frown with gentle fingers. "Come on, let's go." Taking her by the hand, he led her out of the room. "We've still got to stop at the reception desk and pick up our dinner."

A wicker picnic basket was handed over by

the manager, who smiled and said, "Enjoy your evening."

"Which beach are we going to?" Pam asked when Josh led her outside.

"The one right here at our own resort. It's handy, quiet, romantic. What more could we ask for?"

"How about some light?" she suggested as she almost tripped over a flagstone.

"Here. Allow me to help." Josh wrapped one arm around her shoulder and pressed her against him — very snugly against him.

His embrace was more hindrance than help, because Pam now couldn't concentrate at all on walking. The only thing she could think of was the seductively improper way his hand was brushing against the side of her breast. She was nervous and pleased. Excited and dazed.

"It gets even better a little farther along," Josh said as he shifted his hand slightly.

Farther along? She was already pretty far gone! Anticipation was wreaking havoc on her heart rate; her throat was dry and her palms were damp. Maybe she and Josh weren't referring to the same thing. "What's better?"

His smile flashed in the darkness. "Why, the lighting, what else? The resort has very kindly provided some gas-lit torches in their landscaping."

"Torches?" Pam repeated, feeling as if she'd been burned by one.

"Mmm, very effective. Better than candlelight. Wait and see."

Josh was right. The flickering torches cast small pools of light that were big enough for two people if they sat very close to one another. Beyond that the beach was mysterious and shadowy. The sound of the surf was rhythmic and primeval, a litany of power and seduction as the sea tussled with the shore.

"Welcome to my fantasy," he murmured in her ear before releasing her. In a moment he had a blanket spread out on the sand and had tugged her down onto it. Pam automatically kicked off her sandals and reached for the picnic basket. He intercepted her hand and held it in his.

"No, you don't. No peeking," he decreed.

"Spoilsport. I'm starving."

"So am I, Pam." He ran a tempting finger around her lips. "So am I."

She retaliated by nibbling on his finger.

"You keep that up and we're never going to eat," he growled.

The seductive moment was interrupted by the sound of her stomach growling. "I skipped lunch," she explained with a laugh.

"Then I'd better feed you." Josh lowered his hand and gave her a look laced with wicked intimacy. "After all, we don't want any interruptions later."

Later. The possibilities and probabilities filled her with nervous anticipation.

Pam was amazed at the amount of food Josh removed from the picnic basket. There were also crystal wineglasses and a bottle of wine. "All this fit in there?"

"Sure did. Here, hold this." He handed her one of the delicately fluted glasses.

With an expert twist of the corkscrew, Josh opened the wine and poured the sparkling liquid into her glass. "Let's drink a toast to moonlit picnics — the first of many, I hope."

Josh kept his eyes on hers as he raised his glass. Their fingers brushed as their glasses gently clinked. But it was the way he was looking at her that made Pam shiver with excitement. She'd never felt this way before. The looks he gave her were as potent as a kiss, and more powerful than mere words.

Tonight, he promised her with his eyes.

Breathless, Pam was the first to look away.

Josh smiled. He'd seen her hunger, and it wasn't just for food. But he had to feed that hunger before satisfying the other. So he focused his attention on the goodies he'd removed from the picnic basket.

"Let's see what we've got here: chilled lobster, cracked crab legs, jumbo shrimp, carrot

135

sticks and vegetable dip, breadsticks and strawberries."

Everything he'd unpacked was finger food and one look at Josh's face told her he'd planned it that way.

The first offering was innocent enough. Having dipped a breadstick into the dish of whipped butter, Josh held it up to her mouth for her to take a bite.

Pam hesitated for a moment and then leaned forward to accept the offering. Suddenly the common task of eating became a magical experience involving every one of her senses. Food had never tasted so good. But she was aware of much more than the bakery freshness of the breadstick. She was aware of the touch of his fingers as he fed her; the clean scent of his aftershave as it was carried by a balmy sea breeze; the way he watched her as if he was fascinated by her every move; the overwhelming sound of her beating heart. And her sixth sense told her that this was just the beginning!

When Josh had finished feeding her, Pam felt it only fair to return the favor. Dipping a breadstick in the butter, she held it out to him. Josh cupped her hand in his and brought it even closer to his mouth. He then took such a large bite that her fingers were in danger of getting nipped.

"Hey!" she complained with a laugh. "Watch it. I'm rather attached to those fingers."

"So am I," he murmured. "In fact, I'm rather attached to the rest of you too."

"Is that why you tried to take a bite out of me?"

Tugging her hand closer, he kissed the inside of her wrist. "You already know I've got a big appetite."

"Maybe you should wear a sign that says Caution: Don't Feed the Animals."

Josh grinned at her wry comment. "That wouldn't stop you, though, would it? I'll bet you were the type of kid who ignored those signs when you visited the zoo."

Josh was right. As a child, she had ignored the sign and fed the animals anyway. Just as she intended to ignore the tiny voice of warning now. During the past few days she and Josh had shared something special, something that was worth exploring. This was right, she told herself.

"A carrot stick for your thoughts," Josh offered.

"My thoughts are worth a lot more than a carrot stick," she retorted with an arch look that sent Josh's temperature soaring.

He was definitely intrigued. "That good, were they?"

"Yep." She nodded with self-satisfied emphasis.

"Hmm, this sounds promising. Okay, name your price."

"A carrot stick *with* vegetable dip."

Josh's laugh was low and sexy. "I think you're seriously underestimating the value of these thoughts of yours. It sounds to me like they're worth at least a kiss, or two, or three . . ." Moving very slowly, he leaned forward. But instead of kissing her parted lips as she had expected, he smoothed her hair aside so that he could nibble on her ear. He delighted her with tiny kisses and excited her with his darting tongue.

Pam's imagination was racing as wildly as her heartbeat. How would his lips, his tongue, feel on the rest of her body? Josh had only just begun the seduction, and she was already going up in flames. It wasn't fair that she should be the only one feeling this way. It was time she did a little seducing herself.

She chose the cracked crab legs as her tool. Instead of using a fork to dig the tender flesh from the hard shell, she lifted the crab leg to her parted lips and used her teeth to tug the meat gently from its resting place. Her movements were slow and provocative as she drew the meat into her mouth, keeping her eyes on Josh all the while.

He was an appreciative audience. His eyes darkened with hungry fire as she moved on to practice her wiles on a plump jumbo shrimp. First her tongue swirled out to lick a dollop of tangy cocktail sauce from the rounded tip of the seafood. Then her white teeth glided across the shrimp's firm pink flesh before piercing its skin. Her eyes were half-closed with satisfaction as she provocatively nibbled away.

"You're not eating," she chastised him a few moments later. "Come on, try one." She held a shrimp up to his lips. "It's very good."

"You're very good . . . at being naughty," he said slowly.

"Yes, I am," she agreed in a sultry whisper. "So you'd better watch out!"

"Oh, I intend to watch, all right. And touch. And caress."

She waved the shrimp she still held. "And eat?"

"That too." He bit into the shrimp. "Now it's your turn." With tantalizing slowness he reciprocated, sliding bits of lobster into her mouth.

As they continued feeding each other, Josh caressed her cheek, her chin, her throat. Pam responded by kissing him behind his ear, on his chin, along the length of his neck. The seduction was mixed with laughter, especially when they reached the dessert stage and began on the strawberries.

Their fingers collided over the bowl as they both reached for the same strawberry. Instead of taking a berry, Josh brought her hand to his mouth and nibbled on her fingers.

"Hey, watch it!" She tugged her hand away. "That tickles!"

"I am watching, and enjoying what I'm seeing," he said softly. "I like seeing you laugh."

Pam liked what she saw too. Josh had removed his jacket and unbuttoned the top button of his shirt. He smiled at her with his big blue bedroom eyes.

"If you don't want any, then I guess I'll have to eat these all by myself." Selecting a lush strawberry, he dipped it into a small crystal sugar bowl.

Pam complained before he could take a bite of it. "You took the best one!"

"You want this strawberry? Then come and get it." He placed it between his lips but didn't put it into his mouth.

Pam didn't need a second invitation. Kneeling closer, she brought her lips within kissing distance of his. The strawberry now had the rare privilege of being the only thing separating their mouths. The juicy bit of fruit didn't stand a chance.

Her dark eyes alight with laughter, Pam triumphantly claimed her half of the strawberry. Seconds later Josh triumphantly claimed the laughter from her lips. The kiss was even sweeter than the fruit.

At that rate it didn't take long until the strawberries were all gone. So was their patience. Now when their lips merged it was with the sensual expertise of long-time lovers. The preliminary teasing had only made the anticipation — and the enjoyment — greater.

His embrace lured her closer. In a display of gentle strength Josh eased them both down onto the blanket. He covered her, shielding her, seducing her. His hand sensitively trailed over her hip, his touch whisper soft yet erotically intent.

With leisurely skill he continued exploring the soft flesh beneath her caftan. His caresses shifted to her back, to her waist, to the curve of her shoulder. Shivering with pleasure, Pam struggled to undo the buttons of his shirt, but her trembling fingers had difficulty.

Josh suffered from no such handicap as he deftly loosened her caftan's simple tie fastening before sliding the garment first from one shoulder and then from the other. He caressed her with his eyes. In the flickering light from the torches she looked like a sultry goddess, all warm and golden. "I love you like this," he whispered. "You're beautiful, so beautiful . . ."

The rush of the ocean muffled the sounds of Pam's sighs as his tongue ravished her creamy skin. He began at the base of her throat and worked his way lower until he'd reached the warm swell of her breast. There his open-mouthed nibbles dazzled her.

She and Josh heard the sound of approaching voices in the same instant. She voiced a husky objection to the unwelcome intrusion. Josh declared his feelings more succinctly.

Frustrated beyond belief, Pam hurriedly slipped her caftan back on. As they sat up, Josh began shoving things back into the hamper with more haste than caution. Miraculously, nothing broke.

Pam felt as fragile as the delicate crystal Josh had just repacked. Disappointment and resentment burned within her. This beach had been their private idyll, and now it was being encroached upon. Sitting up, she slid her feet back into her sandals. A moment later she looked up to see Josh stashing the hamper behind some nearby rocks and covering it with the blanket.

Before she could ask what he was doing, he approached her and swept her up into his arms. Her startled exclamation was stilled by his kiss. "Let's get out of here."

Looping her arms around his neck, she murmured, "Excellent idea!"

CHAPTER EIGHT

It took Pam a few seconds to realize that Josh was going in the wrong direction.

"Wait, Josh, the hotel is the other way!"

"We're not going back to the hotel. Not yet." He continued walking away from the beach.

"Then where are we going?"

"You'll see. Watch your head," he told her as he ducked beneath some low-hanging palm fronds. "Not much farther now. Ah, here we are. What do you think?"

Pam was speechless. They were standing in the middle of a small Garden of Eden. An enchanting waterfall cascaded into a tiny pool decorated with water lilies. Tropical foliage surrounded the magical oasis, filling the night air with the smell of perfumed flowers. To one side, almost hidden from view by lush bushes, was a cabana.

"There's a key in the pocket of my jeans," Josh said. "See if you can get it out, will you?"

Pam's attention shifted from her surroundings to the man who was still holding her in his arms. "It would be easier if you put me down."

"Easier, maybe, but not half as much fun.

Go ahead, dig in," he invited her.

"Your jeans are so tight I don't think my hand will fit into your pocket," she retorted. She tried and almost got her fingers trapped.

"You're absolutely right," he murmured with a wicked grin. "Come to think of it, I put the key in my jacket pocket at the last minute. Try there."

"Oh, what a pity. And I was just getting used to the lay of the land down here." Her hand shifted in such a bewitching move that Josh almost dropped her.

"It's unfair to torture a defenseless man," he said with a groan. Jiggling her in his arms, he somehow managed to retrieve the key himself and open the door in record time.

The cabana was decorated like something out of the Arabian nights. Huge jewel-colored pillows covered the floor, while sheets of oriental silk hung from the walls. The only light was the moonlight that spilled through the horizontal windows just beneath the roof. No other illumination was needed — the newly risen moon was full and provided a magical aura that couldn't be improved upon.

Pam was almost brought to tears. She'd never seen anything so perfectly romantic.

"What's the matter?" he asked softly. "Don't you like it?"

"I love it."

"Do you want to stay?"

"I want *you*," she whispered.

It was that simple.

Her directness took his breath away. The tempting brush of her lips against his throat destroyed the rest of his self-control. Josh barely had enough presence of mind to lock the door behind them before he captured her wandering lips in a kiss that sizzled.

With her still in his arms, he sank down onto the pillows and lowered her to their welcoming softness. Then he stretched out over her, blanketing her with his strength. Wanting more, she looped her arms around his neck and tugged him closer. Her pliant body shifted to accommodate his, her action intensifying the intimacy of their embrace. She could feel how much he wanted her. His tight jeans did little to disguise that fact.

Pam returned his passion, matched his desire. This time her hands weren't uncertain as she shoved his jacket off his broad shoulders. She transformed the unbuttoning of his shirt into a sensual production, greeting every inch of his bared skin with a seductive rake of her nails. While removing his shirt, she leaned against him, brushing her breasts against his naked chest.

The heat of him burned through her thin cotton caftan. Sliding her hands around to his back, she relished every ridge and contour, exploring him in wonder. When her hands slipped beneath the waistband of his jeans, he muttered her name in hoarse excitement.

His kisses shifted from her mouth to her throat as he quickly freed her from the caftan and tossed the garment into a corner. Now the passage of his hands and mouth over her body was erotically intimate. He handled her with such finesse and skill that she was already burning for him when he removed her lacy blue underwear.

Wild with desire, Pam urged Josh to strip off his jeans and briefs. She was completely out of control, and that realization frightened her in a very primitive way.

As if sensing her fears, her desires, Josh suddenly reversed their positions so that she rested upon him. In doing so, he put the control in her hands.

"Feel what you do to me." He moved against her, tantalizing her with the strength of his arousal. "If you want me, come and get me."

"Josh . . ."

"Sshhh." He soothed her bare thighs with the palms of his hands. "You feel like silk." His caresses shifted to the secret recesses of her body. "Hot silk."

With a cry of pleasure Pam dug her hands

into his shoulders. Leashing his own needs, Josh incited hers. The sensations were so exquisite she could only close her eyes and succumb to them. The ripples of delight grew, lifting her from one peak to another.

He gave her such pleasure that she needed to share it. Her movements became more and more erotic as she drove him as wild as he'd driven her. Pleasing him pleased her.

"Come to me," he rasped, unable to bear her temptation a moment longer.

Pam needed no further bidding. Moving with supple grace, she took all that he offered, welcoming him with fiery hunger. The impact of their union sent a shudder through both of them. Groaning her name, Josh pulled her into the surging urgency of his hips. She matched his rhythm precisely, her eyes half-closed with passionate enjoyment.

Realizing that he couldn't hold out much longer, Josh changed the pattern of their love-making, performing one last rite of magic that sent her over the edge. Gazing down at him with astonished delight, Pam closed her eyes and gave in. The tremors spread swiftly, resulting in a moment of stunning explosion that left her melting in his arms. Her release triggered his own and he, too, surrendered to a force greater than either of them.

Neither spoke for a long time afterward,

but there was no need for words. A look, a touch expressed it all — the wonder, the appreciation. Josh smoothed his hands over her as if wanting to memorize every part of her. Pam did the same to him.

They lay wrapped together, bathed by the moonlight. Josh threaded his fingers through her dark hair, and reading the lingering signs of passion still reflected in her eyes, he murmured, "Do you know one of the first things I noticed about you?"

"That I was about to run you over?" she guessed.

"No."

She ran her finger across his bottom lip. "What then?"

"Your eyes."

She looked up at him. "They're brown."

"I know. And they're beautiful."

He grinned, and she laughed.

"Now it's your turn," he prompted.

She moved against him with languid seduction. "To do what?"

"To tell me what you noticed about me."

She gave him a considering look. "Aside from the fact that I was about to run you over, I'd have to say that I noticed your eyes too."

"They're blue," he mimicked.

"I know. And they're beautiful, too."

He trailed a caressing finger from her wrist

to her elbow. "What else do you like?"

"Maybe I should just show you," she murmured suggestively. And she did — giving pleasure, taking satisfaction with an intensity that left them both dazed.

The next time they spoke, it was in husky whispers.

"How did you find this place?" she asked. "It's perfect."

"So is this place." He kissed the hollow at the base of her throat. "And this." He caressed the valley between her breasts.

Pam never did get around to finding out how Josh had discovered the cabana. She was just glad that he had.

Later they walked back to the hotel like lovers, hands entwined. They shared secret smiles, special looks and kisses that reflected their recent intimacy.

She invited him into her room, and whether she knew it or not, into her heart. Josh spent what was left of the night with her, loving her, being loved by her.

They were sitting in bed, enjoying a midnight snack, when the subject of their first meeting came up again.

"You really made an impact on me," Josh murmured.

"I missed you by a mile," she retorted with a saucy grin he was coming to love.

"You came this close to me." He used his fingers to measure an infinitesimal distance.

"And ever since then you've been trying to get me that close to you again."

"You got that right." Josh complacently ate the last of the grapes they'd been munching on. "And I succeeded, too."

"Now I remember why I was tempted to run you over," she noted dryly.

"Is that all you were tempted to do?"

"No." She paused. "I was tempted to sock you a couple of times."

Josh grinned and tumbled her into his arms. "Haven't you learned yet that it's dangerous to taunt me?"

"I guess I must be a slow learner."

"Oh, I wouldn't say that," he said.

"What's this, praise from the expert?"

"Expert?" he murmured with false modesty. "Shucks, ma'am, I'm just an engineer."

An engineer who specializes in couplings, Pam reminded herself. She didn't want to think about all the practice he must have had perfecting his technique. Shrugging off her dark thoughts, she deliberately changed the subject. "So tell me, did you always want to be an engineer?"

"For a while there it was a toss-up between that and playing football."

"Football? So that's where you got these

muscles. Not from carrying ladies in distress?"

He captured her teasing fingers and ran them over the muscles in question. "Another illusion bites the dust, right?"

"Oh, I wouldn't say that." She shifted her hand so that it rested over his heartbeat. "What made you decide against football?"

"I played while I was at UCLA —"

"Let me guess," she inserted. "Quarterback, right?"

He nodded. "But I quit playing when I graduated. I decided it would be smarter to make a living with my brain instead of breaking my body. Football's a tough business. I didn't want an injury preventing me from being able to throw a football to my son someday."

His words surprised her. She knew he was single now, but she hadn't thought to ask him if he'd been married before. "You've got kids?"

"No, a lot of nieces and nephews, but none of my own. I've never been married. How about you?"

"Same here. Except for the nieces and nephews. I was an only child." Pam didn't want to discuss her own family, so she asked Josh about his.

He amused her with anecdotes and character sketches of his relatives. She enjoyed listening to him. She also enjoyed watching him. Snuggling against him, she was able to study him at close quarters. She noted details and committed them to memory. His right eyebrow quirked up more than his left one did and added that touch of devilment to his expression.

Having run her fingers through his light brown hair, she knew how wonderfully thick it was, but she hadn't realized how short it was actually cut. The style suited him. Not slick or blown dry. Just very masculine.

The more she looked at him, the more fascinated she became — with the way his eyes sloped down at the outside corners; with the fine lines under those eyes, as if he'd spent a lot of time squinting against the sun. Then there was his mouth. His lopsided smile usually hid the more serious side of his nature, but there was a surprising hint of sensitivity in the shape of his lower lip. It wasn't immediately noticeable because of the determined set of his jaw, which was now darkly shadowed with the beginnings of a beard.

Soon looking wasn't enough — she had to touch, too. She scraped a finger lightly over his chin and the line of his jaw. The stubble was slightly abrasive and very sexy.

Josh broke off mid-sentence to press her

hand against his face. He then continued speaking, but Pam couldn't concentrate with him rubbing his unshaven cheek against her palm. The simple gesture was surprisingly erotic.

He could see that she was no longer listening to him. He watched her eyes darken with dreamy passion and waited for her to make her move. He didn't have long to wait. Seconds later her mouth silenced his with a kiss that was warm and enticing.

Pam was thrilled by this newfound freedom to kiss him, to touch him whenever and wherever she pleased. It was gratifying to know that Josh was as affected by her as she was by him. She discovered that the flick of her tongue at the corner of his mouth drove him crazy. He in turn discovered that nibbling on her bottom lip drove her crazy.

"I want you . . . again," he muttered.

"I know." She slid her leg against his.

In one deliberately fluid movement, he rolled her onto her back and made love to her until they were both swept away by passion.

The sun was shining the next time Pam opened her eyes. She blinked at the sight of a very masculine and very bare man strolling across the room toward the bed. "What are you doing up?"

"I'm going to be a gentleman and refrain

from commenting on your very provocative question," he answered. "Whatever happened to *good morning?*"

Pam groaned and would have closed her eyes again, but the sight of him getting dressed was simply too tempting to resist. "What time is it?"

"Seven."

"I guess that means it is morning" — she yawned — "barely."

"Speaking of barely . . ." He sent her a pointed stare.

Looking down, Pam realized that the sheet had slipped to her waist, leaving her breasts bare. Before she could cover herself, Josh stepped forward and did it for her.

Pam was surprised by his action. She would have expected him to make the most of the situation, not put an end to it. Her thoughts turned out to be more prophetic than she knew.

"I woke you up because we need to talk." Josh was unusually serious. "I'm leaving Bermuda today."

His words hit her like a ton of bricks, shattering the fantasy world she'd let herself drift into since last night. Josh was indeed putting an end to it. He was leaving. *Why should he stay?* she questioned numbly. *He'd gotten what he wanted.* Feeling an overwhelming need to get dressed, she got out of bed and pulled on a robe. Her fingers were all thumbs as she attempted to tie a knot in the robe's belt.

"Aren't you going to say something?" he demanded.

Anger came to her rescue. "What do you want me to say? I'm not up on the recommended conversation for the morning after a one-night stand!"

"We shared more than a one-night stand. We shared something special."

"Come on, Josh. You got what you wanted from me. There's no need to keep playing the game. Besides, you're not the only one who has to leave. I have to fly back to Chicago today, too."

Now he was getting angry too. "What do you think I'm saying — thanks for a tumble in the hay; it was fun but I've gotta run now?"

"That's about it."

He grabbed her by the shoulders. "You're wrong. I may have to leave today, but I'll be back in Chicago in ten days."

"So?"

"So I want to see you again."

"Whenever you're in Chicago, right?"

"What's wrong with that?"

"Everything!" She broke away from him. "I'm not a one-night stand, and I'm not available for you whenever you fly into Chicago!"

"I never said you were," he returned impatiently. "I want much more from you than that."

"You want. What about what I want?"

"You want the same thing from me that I want from you," he stated grimly. "A relationship, Pam. Not a one-night stand, not a convenient arrangement."

"What kind of relationship?" she asked warily.

"The serious kind. I won't take more than you're willing to offer, Pam. What are you afraid of?"

"Of you. Of us. This has happened so fast."

"We were meant to be together. Sometimes it happens quickly, sometimes slowly. The amount of time isn't important. The feelings are."

"That's easy for you to say," she retorted. "You've done this a lot. I haven't."

"I've never felt this way before — about anyone."

"You don't have to say that."

He shook his head at the doubt he saw in her eyes. "I'm not just saying it, Pam. I mean it. I don't want this to end." He reached out to cup her chin with his hand. "I don't want to lose you."

Pam blinked back the threat of tears. There was no doubting the sincerity of his claim. "I don't want to lose you either," she admitted.

A moment later she was in his arms. Being held by him always made her heart beat faster, but now it also made her feel cherished. She liked the feeling.

Josh eventually loosened his hold on her. "I've got something for you. Close your eyes and put out your hands."

Tilting her head, she shot him a mischievous look. "Playing touchy-feely again, are we?"

"What a naughty mind you have. I like it." He rewarded her with a kiss. "I also like the perfume you're wearing," he murmured against her lips. "I'm glad you took my advice and bought Seduction." He kissed her again. "I got your present right around the corner from that perfume shop. Now close your eyes and don't open them until I tell you to."

"Have I mentioned that I don't like being told what to do?" she inquired.

"You'll get used to it. Are you going to close your eyes or not?"

"Is that the only way I get to see this present you've bought for me?"

"Yes."

Pam sighed and closed her eyes. A moment later she felt her robe being undone and something soft and cottony being pulled over her head. Her "What . . . ?" was muffled by the material as Josh guided her arms into the sleeves. He provocatively ran his finger around the tip of each breast before tugging the material down and covering them.

"Okay, now open your eyes," he said.

Pam did and looked down at the light blue T-shirt he'd dressed her in. It took her a moment to read the boldly lettered message: SWIMMERS GO THE DISTANCE!

"I think I'm beginning to recognize that stunned look," he said teasingly. "It means you like it, right?"

She nodded.

"Good. Then you won't mind displaying your talent for me."

"I thought I spent the night doing just that," she replied seductively.

"So you did, but I was referring to your swimming talent. I wouldn't mind seeing you in that slinky swimsuit again."

"The feeling's mutual," she murmured with a grin.

They rendezvoused at the hotel's main pool, where Josh challenged her to a race.

"Two laps — first one to touch the wall wins."

Pam nodded and hauled out her swimming cap and racing goggles.

"Hi-tech aids aren't going to help you win," he told her.

"Wanna bet?"

"Sure do. Winner gets to choose the location of our first date in Chicago — agreed?"

"Agreed."

"Fine. On your mark, get set, go!"

Josh won hands down. "We could always do double or nothing," he offered. "We could pick something nice and easy, like a game of croquet."

"I've never played croquet before."

"No problem. I'll teach you."

Josh spent most of his time holding her in his arms, supposedly showing her the proper way to swing the mallet. What he was really doing to her was actually very improper and distracted her so much that she almost hit a passerby with one of her croquet balls.

Josh laughed softly. "Time to quit, I think, before you do anyone bodily harm."

"Me?" She dropped her mallet and turned to face him. "That was all your fault. You're the one who was distracting me."

"Really?" He didn't look the least bit repentant. Sliding his arms around her, he slipped his hands into the back pockets of the shorts she'd put on over her swimsuit. "Is that what I was doing?"

Deciding to fight fire with fire, she melted

against him. "This is what you were doing," she murmured before seductively moving against him.

"Mmmm, nice. You found that distracting?"

"Don't you?"

"I find it to be extremely pleasant."

"Pleasant?" she repeated with pretended outrage.

"How about arousing, stimulating. . . ."

"That's better."

"If it gets any better I'm going to ravish you right here on the grass," he said with a groan.

Pam stepped away from him. "I know just the thing to make you feel better."

His blue eyes were full of warmth. "I'll bet you do."

She nodded. "A nice brisk walk . . ."

"That wasn't quite what I had in mind."

". . . back to our hotel room," she tacked on.

They made one stop on the way, at a rounded arch built of coral stone. "This is a moon gate," Josh announced. "Walking through one brings everlasting luck and happiness."

"Says who?"

"Says me. And says local legend, should you need a second opinion."

"In that case . . ." She nodded her approval of the detour and walked through the moon gate with Josh.

They spent what little time was left in the privacy of his hotel room, making love and fulfilling the happiness promised by the moon gate prophecy. Their imminent departure added a sense of urgency to their caresses, rapidly transporting them to the peak of satisfaction.

Packing was a frantic affair, with Pam jamming things into her suitcase without thought of neatness or order. Her main concern was fitting everything in, and she ended up having to sit on the suitcase to get it closed.

It seemed appropriate that the taxi driver on their last ride turned out to be Trevor, who nodded approvingly. "I knew Bermuda would bring you two together."

All Pam knew was that the taxi ride was over much too quickly. Her flight was already boarding when they arrived at the gate, so there wasn't much time for her and Josh to say their good-byes.

In the end there wasn't any need for words — the fierceness of their embrace spoke for them. Tightening his hold on her, Josh lowered his head and kissed her with hungry passion. His mouth moved over hers as though memorizing the shape and taste of it.

Pam didn't hold back. She put everything into that kiss, showing him how she felt, silently telling him things she hadn't admitted even to herself. She gave him free access to her heart and soul.

His lips left hers with obvious reluctance. His voice was low and raspy as he muttered, "You'd better go while I can still let you."

Pam nodded shakily. Her dark eyes were shadowy, her lips slightly swollen.

He released her, and she stepped away from him. Their eyes clung as Pam took another step backward.

"Ma'am, you're going to miss your flight!" a worried airline official told her.

Pam picked up her hand luggage and dashed to the door.

"I'll be in Chicago in ten days," Josh shouted across the distance now separating them. "Expect me to show up on your doorstep."

"You don't know where I live," she answered him as the airline official hurriedly checked her boarding pass.

"Yes, I do." Josh recited her address and phone number seconds before Pam raced across the tarmac to board the waiting plane.

Pam's flight took off moments later. Looking down, she saw the pastel beauty of Bermuda disappear as the plane headed out over the azure water. She hurt inside, as if part of her heart had been left behind.

She loved him. The realization came to her

right there and then. She loved Josh. For the first time she accepted the fact that he was essential to her happiness. Maybe she'd known it before, only she hadn't wanted to put a label on the excitement, the uncertainty, the delight. It was wonderful, but it was scary.

Pam's soul-searching left her tired by the time the 727 landed in Chicago four hours later. Knowing that Anita would be waiting for her at the agency, Pam took a cab there instead of going directly home.

Anita's expressive face lit up with pleasure when Pam walked in. "Pam, I'm so glad you're back. Look who just got in!" Anita pointed to the man sitting with his back to Pam.

Pam blinked twice, certain she must be seeing things. After chasing him all over Bermuda, Pam had come back to Chicago to find a sheepish-looking Roger sitting in front of her!

He said, "I'm sorry I gave you girls such a scare, but at least I came to my senses before I spent any of the agency's money. I brought it all back, every cent of it! It's right here."

"Grab her, Roger," Anita exclaimed. "I think she's going to faint!"

CHAPTER NINE

Pam felt like she'd stepped into the twilight zone. She was numb all over, and there was a strange buzzing in her ears. Her head was between her knees, and she was sitting in the chair recently vacated by Roger, who'd leapt to catch her before she slumped onto the agency floor.

Roger stood over her, wringing his hands. "I feel so bad about this," he kept saying over and over.

"Pam, are you okay? Do you want a glass of water?" Anita asked from her crouched position beside the chair.

"I'll be all right in a minute," Pam muttered.

"There's no hurry; take it easy." Anita patted Pam's arm reassuringly. "I was surprised when I first saw Roger, too. At least I was already sitting down. But you — you've been running around Bermuda, and then the flight in. No wonder you're . . ."

"A wreck," Pam supplied. Sitting up, she said, "Now let me get this straight. Roger really brought all the money back?"

"That's right," Anita and Roger answered in unison.

"How could you do that?" Pam demanded of Roger.

"I regret taking the money, but you have to understand that I was going through an intense personal crisis."

"No, I meant how could you bring all the money back with you? What about the check?"

Roger looked at her as if she'd gone off the deep end. "What check?"

"The one . . ." Her voice trailed off as she realized, "You don't know anything about it, do you?"

"No."

"*You* brought back the money? All by yourself?"

"That's right," Roger confirmed.

"You never spoke to a man in Bermuda about giving me a check for the missing money?"

"A man in Bermuda? No, I didn't speak to anyone about the money. It's not exactly something you bring up in casual conversation, Pam."

Using twenty-twenty hindsight, she now realized how fishy Josh's story was. Of course Roger wouldn't hand over a check to someone he'd never met, even if Roger had seen Josh accompanying her. It hadn't made sense to her at the time, but she'd allowed herself to be sidetracked by Josh's charm.

"Let's go back to the beginning here," she requested, trying to keep a clear head. "Where did you go when you left the agency with the money, Roger?"

"Bermuda."

"Where in Bermuda?" she demanded impatiently. "I looked all over for you."

"I was staying in a small cottage that belonged to an old college friend of mine," Roger answered.

"Roger was never on that cruise ship," Anita inserted. "I already asked him. But he was at the private country club."

"I was attending a party being given by —"

Pam interrupted him. "By Victor. I know. I was there. I tried to get inside. After searching for three days I finally found someone who recognized your photo, but she said you were using the name of Billy."

"William is my middle name," Roger confessed. "Using Billy was part of the masquerade."

"Yes, well, that masquerade almost got us all into deep trouble," Pam stated bitterly. Masquerades, lies, deceptions — she'd had her fill of them.

"I know, and I'm sorry for putting you two through such a difficult time. But look on the bright side. At least I didn't spend any of the money, and Anita assures me that the clients were never even aware of its temporary disappearance." Roger paused and self-consciously ran a hand through his thinning red hair. "I want to thank you both for having faith in me when I'd lost faith in myself."

"That's okay, but please don't ever do anything like that again," Anita pleaded.

"You've got my word on it. Living the high life isn't all it's cracked up to be."

"Most things aren't," Pam noted wearily. Love certainly wasn't.

Roger took a look at his watch. "It's after closing time. Let's lock up here, go across the street and drop this money in the bank's night deposit slot before it causes any more trouble."

It had already caused more trouble than Roger could possibly know, Pam thought to herself. She was still feeling shell-shocked as she let herself into her apartment half an hour later. The living room looked the same — she even looked the same when she caught her reflection in the mirror. But she felt like a stranger in her own home. So much had happened to her since she'd left Chicago . . . was it only five days ago?

She wasn't the same person now that she had been then. As Pam felt the tears running down her face, she remembered telling Josh she never cried. And she hadn't, much, until she'd met him. Now look at her. A nervous wreck over a guy who'd made love to her and lied to her.

At least she hadn't told him she loved him; she'd never spoken the words out loud, even to herself. Of course Josh had never said he loved her either. He'd said he cared for her; he'd said he'd see her in Chicago in ten days. But then he'd also said Roger had given him a twenty-thousand-dollar check to give to her. Where did the deception end? Had everything been a lie? And what about the check? What was she supposed to do with it? Was it even real, or as phony as Josh's stories?

The questions kept tumbling through her mind. What if Roger hadn't returned of his own volition? What if Pam had gotten back and cashed the check she'd thought was from Roger, only to have it bounce? The possible repercussions of such an action made her grow cold. The consequences would have been disastrous.

But what if the check is real? she asked herself. Had she been paid for services rendered? Was that why Josh had done it? *Twenty thousand seems pretty exorbitant for one night,* she thought to herself with a hysterical sob.

When the phone began to ring she was tempted to ignore it, but its persistence finally forced her to pick it up. She could tell right away that the call was long distance; the static on the line told her that much.

"Pam, it's Josh." Even from halfway around the world his voice sounded warm and intimate. "I'm calling from Heathrow Airport in London. I'm changing planes, but I wanted to make sure you got in okay." He paused, obviously waiting for her to say something. When she didn't, he demanded, "Can you hear me?"

"I hear you." Her anger carried through the phone lines.

"Pam, is something wrong?"

"You might say that," she retorted sarcastically. "You'll never believe who was sitting in the travel agency waiting for me when I got in. My boss — Roger. With all the agency's money."

Josh swore. "Pam, listen —"

"No, you listen! Is that check you gave me kosher? Or is it as fake as you are?"

"The check is real. It was prepaid."

"You make a habit of this, do you? Giving your women twenty-thousand-dollar tokens of affection? Lying to them?"

"We can't talk about this on the phone," he said.

"You got that right," she shot back. "We can't talk, period. Give me the address of your

170

company headquarters and I'll mail the check back to you!"

"Forget it. I'll see you when I get back to Chicago. Until then, know that I did what I did for your own good. I care about you, Pam. I —" He was cut off by the beep-beep-beep signaling that his time was up, and he was disconnected.

The phone rang again a few minutes later, but Pam refused to answer it.

So Josh had done it for her own good, had he? It all sounded so terribly familiar. She'd heard that excuse over and over while she was growing up. The fact that Josh had used the exact same words shook her deeply. She'd stopped playing those power games when she'd left home.

Her adoptive father had been a master of manipulation. He'd given new meaning to the word *strict* but had justified his behavior by stating that he had her best interests at heart. She'd soon learned that he had no heart. He'd simply enjoyed the power of controlling another human being. Now here she was again, wanting love from a man who wanted to control her. The tears began once more.

The pain of Josh's deception remained long after she'd finally cried herself out. How easily she'd been deceived by Josh's wicked grin and bedroom eyes. How quickly she'd forgotten her initial wariness. How long would it take her to get over him? she wondered miserably.

She got little sleep that night. Instead she sat, drained and empty, staring into the darkness and waiting for the dawn.

Anita knew something was wrong the minute Pam walked into the office the next morning. "Bad night?"

Pam nodded but didn't volunteer any information.

Seeing the pain in Pam's eyes, Anita didn't pursue the subject.

Desperate for something to take her mind off Josh, Pam welcomed the pile of work sitting on her desk waiting for her attention. Itineraries needed to be arranged, bookings confirmed. It worked somewhat. The morning passed quickly, but there was a lull during the afternoon.

Anita used the opportunity to confront Pam. "You look awful," she said with the bluntness of a friend. "Something obviously happened while you were in Bermuda. Do you want to talk about it?"

Pam had never been one to keep her emotions under control for long. So she confided in Anita. Knowing Anita's recent divorce had given her a low opinion of men in general, Pam never expected that Anita would come to Josh's defense.

"Men are creeps," Anita said. "But this one sounds better than most. It sounds like he was trying to help you, not hurt you."

"He deceived me. Deliberately."

"There are levels of deception. Deceiving someone by cheating on her with another woman, like my rotten ex-husband did to me, well that's a major deception. Lying about being married or having a communicable social disease, those are major deceptions. This . . . I don't know. I've never heard of a guy giving someone a check for twenty thousand dollars." The amount was more than Anita's annual salary. "It's still kind of hard to believe."

"I can't believe he did it either," Pam muttered. "But I realize I really don't know much about Josh Phillips. A week ago I didn't even know he existed."

"And now you can't think of anything else." Seeing Pam's mutinous look, she said, "Well, it's true, isn't it? You've been acting strangely ever since you got back from Bermuda."

"I only got back yesterday, you know. It takes awhile to recover from the shock of having your boss take off with your clients' money," Pam retorted. Roger was out of the office for the afternoon, attending a presentation by a group of tour operators, so she felt safe putting the blame on him.

"Roger doesn't have anything to do with it," Anita stated.

"Yes, he does. If he hadn't flown the coop for Bermuda, I never would have met Josh and I never would have fallen —" Pam stopped herself before she said the words.

"Go on. You never would have fallen what?"

"Never would have fallen for his act," she substituted.

"It wasn't just an act," Anita said. "He put his money where his mouth is."

Thinking about Josh's mouth reminded her of the way they'd made love, and that was something Pam couldn't afford to remember. "I don't care why he did it. The bottom line is that he lied to me and deceived me. No check, no matter how large, can make up for that!"

"He really got to you, didn't he?" Anita noted softly.

"It was a vacation fling, nothing more than that." *Maybe if I say that often enough, I'll be able to convince myself.*

"You seem awfully upset for it to have been just a fling. You've dated a lot of men before and never gotten this intense."

"That's because those men weren't as impossible as Josh is!" Pam threw down the pencil she'd been playing with and began pacing the small office. "I should have known better. I let myself be swept off my feet. He was trouble from the word go. I could tell from the first second I laid eyes on him. You know the type — sun-bleached hair, blue eyes, brawny muscles. Confident, smooth, in control. He tried to take charge of me right from the beginning, hauling me off to that doctor's office."

"What doctor's office?" Anita demanded, trying to keep up with Pam's tirade.

"I'd had a slight accident with the moped I'd rented, and Josh insisted on taking me to a doctor even though I didn't need one."

"You never told me you were in an accident. When did this happen?"

"A few hours after I arrived there," Pam replied. "That's how I met Josh. He was jogging along the road and I almost hit him."

"Sounds like you two were on a collision course right from the beginning."

Pam considered Anita's description and decided it was an apt one. She sure felt like she'd been hit by a truck.

Pam went home after work, dreading another sleepless night. So she called a friend and went out for dinner and to a movie. She fell asleep during the feature's most exciting chase scene. She dreamed about Josh. She resented being shaken awake by her friend. Her dreams had been much simpler than reality was.

Pam waited all week for Josh to call her again. She didn't know whether to be relieved or disappointed that he didn't. It felt like she was waiting for the other shoe to drop.

The week was a busy one, with several people calling wanting to take spur-of-the-moment trips. A little over a week after her return from Bermuda, Pam was in the back room, getting brochures from the files, when she heard the chime on the door announcing the arrival of a client.

"Pam, there's someone here to see you," Anita called out.

"I'll be there in a minute." *It's probably Mrs. Griswald,* Pam thought to herself. The elderly woman had mentioned stopping in to pick up her tickets to Las Vegas today.

It wasn't Mrs. Griswald. It was Josh. An impatient, tired, angry and strangely uncertain-looking Josh.

His first words to her were, "Do you know how many Global Travel Agencies there are in the city of Chicago?"

"No. And I don't really care." She reached for her swivel desk chair and sat down before she fell down.

"Oh, you care all right, Pam. If you didn't, you wouldn't still be so angry with me. And I wouldn't have gone without sleep for three nights just so that I could get back here earlier."

"I see you still think you have all the answers," she retorted. She must have imagined the uncertainty. Josh was obviously as impossibly confident as ever.

"Do you want to fight here, or would you prefer that we do it in the privacy of your apartment?"

Pam had no intention of letting him near her apartment. "I'm done fighting with you."

"So what do you plan on doing now, ripping the check into little pieces and flinging them in my face?"

That was exactly what she was tempted to do, but she refused to give him the satisfaction of being right. Instead she turned the tables on him. "Now why would I want to do a dumb thing like that?" she asked. "Apparently you've got money to blow, and apparently you believe I earned that twenty thousand, so I went out and blew it all — on a new Ferrari!"

Josh's blue eyes opened wide before narrowing again. "Nice try, but I happen to own a Ferrari and I know they cost over sixty thousand, not twenty thousand."

"Okay, the truth is I don't want your money — I don't want anything to do with you!"

"That's not the truth at all, and you know it. All right — you're hurt, you're angry, I can understand that. I can explain —"

"I don't need an explanation. When a man gives a woman a check for that amount of money, the intention is pretty obvious. You were paying me off."

"I was trying to help you."

"By lying to me?"

"Maybe you two would rather be left alone?" Anita inserted uncomfortably.

Pam and Josh didn't even hear her.

"Given the circumstances, lying was understandable and forgivable," he maintained.

"Lying to me under any circumstances is unforgivable."

"So you're going to stay mad at me for the rest of your life?" He glared at her.

"Probably, yes!" She glared right back.

Unnoticed, Anita gathered her purse and slipped out of the office.

"I did it for your own good!" Josh shouted.

His words uncovered old wounds. "God protect me from things done for my own good," she stated bitterly.

"What's that supposed to mean?"

"It means that I've had it with men telling me they know what's best for me! I've heard it all before. My father claimed he was being strict for my own good. I was supposed to obey him without question because he knew what was best for me. The truth was that he enjoyed bullying me." Pam didn't realize she was shaking until she'd stopped speaking.

Josh's face was taut with emotion. "Is that why you're taking this so hard? Because of your father?"

"Don't you dare stand there psychoanalyzing me! Don't stand there, period." She fumbled with the lock on her bottom desk drawer. Yanking it open, she removed the piece of paper that had caused her so much pain. "Here" — she shoved the check at him — "take it and leave."

"It's not that simple, Pam." He took the check, tore it in pieces and dropped it in the trash. "All right, I'll admit my methods may have been wrong, but my intentions were good. I'm sorry I lied to you. I can't go back and change what's already been done. If you'd talked to me more, told me something about your background, I wouldn't have done what I did."

"Oh, so now it's all my fault, is that it?"

"No, that's not it."

"What did you think you were doing, reimbursing me for a night in the sack?"

Josh grabbed her by the shoulders and shook her. "Don't say that! Don't even think it. I gave you the check for this agency, so you could replace the deposits of all those clients you told me about — the ones who'd saved all their lives for a vacation. I had no way of knowing your boss would reappear. I planned on hiring a detective agency to try and track him down. I was trying to save your job and I was trying to prevent you from continuing your wild chase after Bass. Okay, so the idea wasn't the best, but it was the only solution I could come up with. Time was running out for me. I knew I'd be leaving Bermuda soon . . ."

"So you arranged things in your best interest. If there's a problem, you just lie and buy your way out of it. Don't try telling me you gave me that check on my clients' behalf. You did it because it was the most convenient way of getting what you wanted. And you're the type of man who always gets what he wants, aren't you, Josh? You wanted me, so you made arrangements to get me. Whatever the price."

"I'm not your father, Pam," he said quietly. "Stop convicting me for his crimes."

His accusation made her furious. "You don't know the first thing about me!"

"I know that I still want you."

"There you go again. What *you* want. Well, I've got news for you, Josh. I don't care what you want anymore. That's your problem."

Her problem was going to be getting over him. Even now she was still painfully aware of everything about him. It looked like he'd come straight from the airport. His suit was crumpled, his tie loosened. He hadn't shaved, and his blue eyes were red-rimmed with exhaustion. Pam steeled herself to remain unmoved by his appearance. It didn't matter how he looked; she had to protect herself at all costs. Josh was simply the wrong man for her. She had to keep reminding herself of that fact.

Josh stared at Pam's face, trying to read the thoughts going through her head. She looked so cool and crisp in that white dress she was wearing. But her eyes were stormy with emotion, and they gave him hope.

"We shared something special in Bermuda, Pam. I'm not walking away from that. I'm not going to lose you."

"You already have."

"You don't really mean that."

"There you go again," she said, her temper flaring. "Telling me what I mean, telling me what I feel."

"Because you won't tell me your feelings."

"You want to hear about my feelings? Fine. I feel like I've been deceived."

"I can understand that," he said softly, "and I want to make it up to you."

"Then leave me alone." Her voice was getting desperate now.

"I can't do that, Pam. I made a mistake and I can't change that, but I'm not giving up on us. Not by a long shot. We were meant to be together. I know that and I plan on making sure you know it, too."

"You're wasting your time."

"I don't think so. You see, Pam, I'm going to woo you and court you until you give in."

"I'll never give in!" she vowed.

"We'll see."

Pam didn't want to see, she didn't want to hear, she didn't want to feel anything for Josh. If only it were that easy.

CHAPTER TEN

True to his word, Josh began his battle to regain her affections the very next morning. Pam arrived at work to find a floral arrangement of wild orchids on her desk.

"The siege begins," she muttered to herself. She had no doubt that the flowers were from Josh.

"Aren't you going to read the card?" Anita asked.

"No." Pam took the tiny envelope and dropped it into her trash can. She then removed her jacket and arranged it on the back of her chair. She'd deliberately put on one of her favorite outfits today; a dark teal suit with an aqua jacquard silk blouse. The boost to her self-confidence helped. She was a strong woman; she'd be able to resist whatever plan Josh might devise. Or so she kept telling herself.

But Josh's unopened card lay in her wastebasket like a homing device, drawing Pam's attention to it again and again. She'd rearranged her desk accessories and sharpened a dozen pencils before finally giving in. "Oh, all right!" she muttered as if answering a persistent call. She would open the card, read it, and then rip it into tiny pieces.

Only it didn't work out that way. Because there was nothing written on the card. She turned it over twice. It was blank.

She was still trying to figure out if the florist had made a mistake when the agency's glass door was shoved open and a messenger announced, "Special delivery for Pam Warner."

"Over here."

Obviously in a hurry, the young man tossed down an envelope bearing the word *urgent.* "Sign here." He shoved a clipboard at Pam.

"This is getting interesting," Anita murmured as Pam hastily scrawled her signature. "What do you think it is?"

"It's probably the travel documents for that couple going to China this fall," Pam answered. But one look at the return address told her it was from Josh. Inside were several sheets of paper, all blank. Attached to them was a self-sticking note that said:

> This is how I feel without you —
> Blank, empty, lonely.
>
> Josh

Pam drew in a shaky breath. This was going to be tougher than she'd thought.

More flowers arrived the next morning.

"I'm impressed," Anita declared.

"I'm not." This was only day two of the siege and already Pam's nerves were shot. "Haven't you ever heard of men who only want what they can't have?"

"You really think Josh is chasing you because you said no?" Anita asked.

"Yes."

"And you think that's the only reason?"

Pam shrugged.

"What if he's telling the truth? What if he is sorry about misleading you and really does care?"

"I don't know." Pam sat down at her desk and began shuffling a stack of travel itineraries. "I don't want to think about it."

"I don't think Josh is going to let you forget about it, or him."

Pam sighed and shoved the papers aside. "What did you think of him?"

"I may not be the most objective person to ask," Anita told her. "You know that I haven't exactly been enamored of men since my divorce."

"It still hurts, doesn't it?"

Anita nodded. "I can understand your wanting to avoid that kind of pain. It will be quite a while before I feel able to trust again. But there's a difference between ducking after you've been hit once and ducking just in case someone might punch you. I know you had a hard time while you were growing up and it's natural that you would be cautious. Just don't let that caution stand in the way of your happiness."

"Does that mean you liked Josh?"

"I only saw him for a few minutes. Physically, he's a hunk, and those eyes of his are real sexy. But what really struck me was the way he was looking at you. I don't know how to describe it exactly, but it was definitely something special."

That's how Josh had described what they'd shared in Bermuda — something special. Pam reminded herself that Josh was a pro at creating an image, and he was an expert at handling women. Naturally he'd have the long, lingering looks down pat by now. But no matter how hard she tried to convince herself, she couldn't completely dismiss Anita's observation from her mind.

The next day there was another floral delivery, this time a blooming potted hibiscus bush. The blossoms were a deep coral and delicately marked. "These looked like something special," Josh had written. "So are you."

"It's beginning to look like a florist's shop in here," Roger noted. "What's going on?"

"A budding romance," Anita quipped.

"We haven't had much of that around here lately," Roger murmured.

"I know. We haven't had anything this romantic happen since Pam booked that friend of hers on a bus tour of Europe." Anita sighed enviously. "You remember the story, don't you? The woman's first trip abroad and she meets a race car driver, marries him, and moves to Monte Carlo."

Pam hastily set the record straight. "In the first place, my friend Mary Ellen knew Ty before he joined her on that tour. They'd fallen in love when they were teenagers. So their situation is nothing like mine. And in the second place, Josh is not being romantic. He's just going after something he wants."

"And that's not romantic?"

"Sometimes it is. Other times it's a real pain."

"Like those cases where the guy rents a billboard and puts some woman's name on it?"

Pam looked horrified. "You don't think Josh will do that, do you?"

"I'll tell him not to."

"You've talked to him?"

"Sure," Anita cheerfully confessed. "He calls here every afternoon to find out how you liked his flowers."

"Why didn't you tell me?" Pam demanded.

"Because he wasn't calling you. Josh is

187

doing his homework first, he says. So he's been asking me for advice."

"Anita! That's not fair. You're not supposed to take his side in this. You're supposed to be my friend."

"I am your friend. That's why I'm helping him. I think he's good for you."

"Well, I don't. And I'd appreciate it if you wouldn't encourage him to keep doing this."

"If you ask me, Josh doesn't need any encouragement," Anita retorted. "He's going to chase you whether I help him or not."

Pam had to admit that Anita was probably right, but that didn't make her feel any better. The lies Josh had told her and his conviction that he'd done what was best for her had shaken her trust in him. Why couldn't Anita understand that?

Pam's feeling of being ganged up on was reinforced by Roger later that afternoon. "Great work, Pam."

Surprised by his air of jolly satisfaction, she said, "Are you talking about something specific or just giving me a general compliment?"

"I'm talking about the new corporate account that friend of yours got for us."

"What friend of mine?" Pam asked, even though she was afraid she already knew.

"The one who's been sending all the flowers. It seems he recommended us to an engineering firm he's done work with. And then there's an accounting firm whose employees do a lot of business traveling. They said Josh Phillips had recommended us to them too."

"Has Josh talked to you?" Pam demanded.

Roger shifted uncomfortably.

"Well, has he?"

"Is that any way to speak to your boss?" Roger protested with a shake of his head.

"You're avoiding my question."

"Okay, okay. Yes, I have talked to Josh and I appreciated his frankness."

Pam didn't like the sound of that. "What'd he say?"

"That he was angry at the way I put the future of this agency in jeopardy."

She was furious. "He had no right saying that!"

"At first I was surprised and concerned that you'd told somebody outside the agency about what happened."

"I can explain about that, Roger —"

"No need. Josh already said he made you tell him. And he was right. My actions did put us all in jeopardy. He told me what trouble you got yourself into chasing me. I'm just glad he was there to help you."

"Help me!" Pam fumed. "If it hadn't been for his interference, I would have found you at the country club. But no, he had to show up out of nowhere and haul me away!"

"Funny, that's what Josh said you'd say. But you could have gotten into serious trouble if you'd been caught trespassing, Pam. He explained how you wouldn't give up the search, how you were convinced that I wasn't the type of man who'd really steal our clients' money. He said he'd do anything to get a woman to have that kind of faith in him."

Pam was shaken by this revelation. She'd never considered the possibility that Josh might need her, other than in a purely physical sense. But could she believe him? Would she ever be able to believe him again?

It was frightening to realize that even though she hadn't seen Josh or spoken to him in two days, he'd still managed to influence her. By successfully recruiting both Anita and Roger into joining his crusade, Josh had surrounded her with a constant barrage of propaganda — all in his favor.

Pam soon began looking forward to the upcoming weekend; at least then she'd be able to escape Roger's and Anita's constant comments. Although the flowers kept coming, Josh still hadn't called her, and Pam was getting antsy waiting to see what he'd do next.

All day Saturday she waited for a call or a knock on her door. She would have gone out, but she refused to let Josh scare her out of her own apartment. So she stayed home and did some belated spring cleaning. She took a break late in the afternoon for her customary walk to the corner newsstand, where she always bought the Chicago *Sun-Times*.

Pam knew the vendor by name and often stopped to chat. Aristotle Andropolois, officially known as Art, was a former weight lifter who still looked the part even though it had been a good twenty years since he'd owned his body-building parlor.

"How's it goin'?" Art asked.

"So-so," Pam replied.

"I got something special for you," Art announced with his slight Greek accent.

Pam's heart lurched. She was in pretty bad shape when two simple words — *something special* — even spoken by the corner newspaper vendor — made her . . . what? Excited, nervous?

Telling herself not to be ridiculous, Pam asked, "What have you got?"

"Your newspaper. I saved one special for you. I know how upset you get when I sell out."

See? Boy, are you getting paranoid. She took the folded paper he handed her. "Wait a minute — this is too skinny to be my newspaper."

"Read it," Art commanded.

The banner headline proclaimed TRAVEL AGENT STEALS ENGINEER'S HEART!

Pam's eyes opened wide. "How . . . ?"

"You gonna stay mad at that nice young man after he ran here to give that present to you?" Art demanded.

"The least you can do is say thank you," Josh murmured from behind her.

She turned to find Josh standing there, wearing a pair of sexy running shorts. He was not wearing a shirt. His bare skin gleamed in the sunlight and was covered with a thin layer of sweat that made him look like an oiled teak carving.

Pam suddenly found it hard to breathe. She couldn't take her eyes off him. How could she have forgotten that golden hair on his chest?

"Is something wrong?" he asked. Following the direction of her stare, he added, "Don't tell me the sight of my manly chest has made you speechless?"

Gathering her scattered wits, Pam looked at the newspaper headline and then back at him. "Your heart looks fine to me," she noted tartly.

"You can't tell just by looking. You have to feel it to really know," he murmured.

"Forget it," she shot back.

"I can't forget it. I can't forget how good things were between us. Can you?"

Pam refused to answer his question.

"I didn't think so. So what are we going to do about it?"

"*We're* not going to do anything. I'm going back to my apartment."

"You're not going to send away a thirsty man without even offering him a glass of water, are you?"

"As long as you know that water is all I'm offering," she declared.

Walking the half-block back to her apartment building, Pam wondered what she was letting herself in for. *Nothing,* she told herself. *I'll give him a glass of water and send him on his way.* She refused to be intimidated by the fact that he was only half-dressed and that she wasn't wearing very much herself. Her flirty print shorts and cropped short-sleeve top were perfectly respectable. It was Josh's appraisal that made her feel almost naked. It was a skill he had.

Following her inside the second-story apartment, Josh looked around with interest. The apartment was sparsely and inexpensively furnished. But the tropical-patterned throw pillows, travel posters, and abundant greenery gave the place a light and airy feeling.

"Nice, very nice."

"I'm so glad you approve." Pam's comment was meant to be sarcastic but instead it sounded uncertain and breathless. "Did you want ice in your water? Or I've got fresh lemonade, if you'd prefer some of that. I just squeezed the lemons this morning." *What did you say that for? You know that giving Josh an inch is like giving him a mile.*

Sure enough, Josh joined her in the kitchen. "Lemonade sounds good."

He looked good, standing there on her cracked linoleum floor.

"I hope I'm not interrupting anything?" he asked with surprising courtesy.

"No, I was just about to make a late lunch."

"I haven't eaten yet, either."

The next thing she knew Pam was asking if he wanted to stay for lunch. "It's nothing fancy, just ham sandwiches," she added hastily, already regretting the invitation.

"I don't need fancy, Pam. I need you."

Pam almost dropped the bottle of mayonnaise she'd just removed from the refrigerator.

"Here, let me help you." Josh stepped forward to take the bread, tomato, and head of lettuce she'd already piled into her arms. When his fingers inadvertently brushed against her breast, Pam trembled and her mouth grew dry. She was stunned by the longing the brief contact provoked. Retreating to a safe distance, she attempted to recover her equilibrium and waited for Josh to make some comment.

But he didn't push the situation. He simply set the sandwich fixings on the kitchen counter and pitched in preparing lunch. She hadn't expected him to know his way around a kitchen and was surprised to learn that he was apparently quite familiar with the finer points of cooking. He even knew which knife to use when cutting a tomato so that it didn't end up a squashed mess.

Pam soon found herself wondering what it would be like having him help her make lunch every Saturday afternoon. Disturbed by the direction of her thoughts, she shook her head, as if that would clear her thinking. It didn't.

Pam let Josh do most of the talking as they sat down and began eating their lunch. She was too distracted to make any intelligent replies anyway. Certain that Josh's half-dressed body was at fault, she retrieved a large T-shirt from her closet and handed it to him. "Here, put this on."

Josh looked at it and grimaced. "Pink isn't really my color." But he did put it on.

The shirt didn't help as much as she'd hoped it would. Now he looked like Don

Johnson from "Miami Vice."

"Satisfied?" Josh inquired. His right brow was lifted in the mocking gesture she knew so well.

"It will have to do," she muttered. A rumble of thunder made her jump.

"Sounds like there's a storm coming," Josh noted. "Remember getting caught in the rain when we were in Bermuda?"

Pam remembered only too well. "How about dessert?" she asked abruptly.

"But you haven't finished your sandwich yet."

"I'm a big girl now; I don't have to eat everything on my plate anymore," she stated.

"Oh, I wouldn't say you were *big*," he replied. "I'd say you were shaped just right."

Pam didn't say a word as she poured a carton of whipping cream into a bowl and turned on the hand mixer. The high whine of the kitchen appliance made conversation difficult, which was fine with her.

Josh approached her, holding the loaf of bread. He had to come very close to be heard over the mixer and the increasing thunder. "Where do you want this?"

Before Pam could answer, there was a flash of lightning, instantly followed by a clap of thunder that sounded like it was directly above them. The electricity flickered and went out, throwing the kitchen into eerie gloominess.

"Steady," Josh murmured as Pam jumped nervously. "It's just a storm. It'll be over soon." He took the mixer out of her hand and set it on the counter. A second later his arms had stolen around her and tugged her close. "Maybe this is a sign from above that we're meant to be together."

Pam lifted her head to protest such a ridiculous suggestion, but the words were stolen from her lips as Josh leaned down and kissed her. Her opposition melted like ice cubes in August. The only thing she could think of was how good it felt to be in his arms again. She succumbed to the pleasure and responded to the kiss. Her lips parted, allowing the tempting entry of his tongue. Hers was there to greet it, and the ensuing tussle was blatantly evocative.

The next thing Pam knew there was a whirring in her ears. She ignored it, but there was no ignoring the feeling of being splattered with something wet. Gasping in surprise, she broke away from Josh to find that the power had been restored and that she'd left the hand mixer on. The beaters, which had been full of stiffened whipping cream, were spewing their contents all over her, Josh, and the newly cleaned kitchen!

"Oh, no!" Pam had to tug the cord from the wall outlet to get the mixer to stop its maniacal dance on the countertop.

"This is an unusual way to serve strawberry shortcake," Josh noted with a grin as he wiped a dab of whipping cream off his arm. "Hold the strawberries and the shortcake. Quite inventive. I like it," he murmured as he pulled her close to lick a dollop of whipped cream from her cheek.

Pam trembled. She couldn't think straight when he was doing such wickedly enjoyable things to her. He was seducing her all over again. His hand slipped beneath her cropped top to caress her back, while his lips traveled across her face. His fingers stroked her as he murmured in her ear, "I want you to remember what we shared in Bermuda, Pam, what we could be sharing again." To her surprise, he then released her and gave her a smoldering look. "You think about it. I'll see you tomorrow." Then he was gone.

"That's what you think!" Pam threw a roll of paper towels across the kitchen. She was not going to melt and give in. Muttering under her breath, she began the lengthy cleaning-up effort. Whipped cream had splattered on the ceiling, the hood over the stove, even the top of the refrigerator. As she worked, Pam resolutely refused to dwell on the way she'd responded to Josh's kisses. He hadn't won yet.

Sunday was a gorgeous day, and Pam was not about to sit around her apartment waiting for Josh to show up. Now that her apartment was clean, her car was next on the list. So she drove her three-year old Mustang to the do-it-yourself car wash that was set up in the parking lot of St. Michael's church. The three-dollar fee went to charity and got you a bucket full of soapy water, a sponge, and access to a hose.

The turnout was good, which was why Pam didn't realize Josh was watching her until it was too late. She was leaning across the hood of her car, scrubbing a stubborn mark that was partially out of reach, when someone commented, "Lady, those cutoffs ought to be illegal!"

The soapy sponge fell from her fingers and slid down the sloping hood as Pam swiveled to face Josh. "Stop sneaking up on me all the time!" At least today he was wearing a shirt, although the tank top did more to accentuate his muscles than to cover them.

"Don't stop. I was just enjoying the view." His eyes dropped to her tanned legs.

"How did you find me?" she demanded.

"I'd recognize your legs anywhere."

"I doubt that you could see them from my apartment; it's three blocks away from here."

"You're right. Actually I was running along this block on my way to your apartment when I caught sight of this gorgeous brunette sprawled across the hood of a red car. I saw the long sexy legs and I knew it had to be you."

"Likely story," she retorted.

"It's the truth."

"You wouldn't know the truth if it came up and bit you," she countered. Giving him a dirty look, she reached for the roll of paper towels she'd brought with her and began drying the hood she hadn't even finished washing.

"Temper, temper. You're going to rub a hole through the finish. And you missed a spot in the center there."

"Are you going to stand there criticizing me?"

"No, I'm going to help you." Josh held up his own bucket and sponge. Ignoring her sputtering protests, he began working, starting with the spot on the hood that she hadn't been able to reach.

Pam moved out of his way and began working on the car's trunk. Her progress was slow because she kept pausing to steal quick looks at Josh. If her cutoffs were illegal, then his running shorts ought to be outlawed! Today he was wearing a black pair, and when he leaned over she saw how strong and muscular his thighs really were.

Even though the sunshine wasn't that intense, Pam suddenly felt very, very hot. Trying to cool off, she undid the bottom buttons of her camp shirt and tied the two ends together into a knot just beneath her breasts. But when she noticed the way Josh was watching her, her temperature soared again. His knowing grin only made matters worse.

The message he was sending came in loud and clear. *I'm getting to you. I'm the one making you all hot and bothered.*

Pam grabbed the plastic hose that lay nearby and responded with action instead of words or thoughts. Putting her thumb over the hose nozzle, she aimed a powerful spray of water straight at him.

Surprised, Josh yelled, "What are you doing?"

"You looked like you needed to cool down."

"Allow me to return the favor," he replied with a wolfish smile. Using a fake rush, he side-stepped the spray and got close enough to grapple over the hose. In the process they both got soaking wet.

"So I'm the one who needed cooling down?

How about you?" he challenged.

"Let go!" It was hard for her to keep hold of the hose when she was laughing so hard.

"Why? So you can douse me again? No way."

One minute Pam and Josh were playing tug of war with the hose and the next they were staring into each other's eyes, all thought of fun and games gone.

The sounds and people around them faded away, leaving only the two of them suspended in time. Pam felt strangely disoriented as she stared into Josh's intense blue eyes. Something important was about to happen, she could feel it.

And she was right. Josh stood in the middle of that chaotic parking lot and finally declared his feelings for her. "I love you, Pam."

CHAPTER ELEVEN

Pam was stunned. Josh loved her? Did he really mean it? Or had he only said it so that she'd come back to him? Had he loved her when he lied to her? So many questions. She searched Josh's face for the answers.

He didn't look away but met her gaze with warm reassurance. For once his blue eyes were serious, and he was looking at her as if she were the most precious thing in his life. Even so, she was still wary, afraid to trust him again. Gradually it dawned on her that they were both still holding the hose, even though the water was now flowing harmlessly onto the warm pavement.

"We're all wet," she noted inanely.

"Did you hear what I said?"

"I heard you." She let go of the hose and took a step backward. "I just don't know whether or not to believe you."

Tossing the hose aside, Josh wrapped his fingers around her shoulders. "What have I got to do to convince you? You wanted honesty, so I gave you honesty. I do love you. I could have planned a romantic evening with candlelight, but instead I blurt it out in the middle of a crowded parking lot. Surely that tells you something?"

"Maybe you realized that telling me in a crowded parking lot would be more effective than telling me over a candlelit dinner," she returned.

"How the hell am I supposed to know which way would be more effective?" he demanded in exasperation. "Apparently no matter what I do, you think that I've planned it all out ahead of time. Am I right?"

"Aren't you always right?"

He frowned and gave her a gentle shake. "Why do you do that?"

"Do what?"

"Get defensive with me." He traced a soothing finger down her throat. "I'm not going to hurt you."

"You already have."

"You've hurt me too," he returned quietly. "That surprises you, doesn't it? It shouldn't. Our relationship is a two-way street — the feelings work both ways. If I didn't love you, why do you think I've kept chasing you?"

"Because I'm a challenge to you."

Josh swore under his breath and released her. He impatiently wiped the remaining drops of water from his face before giving her a challenging stare. "You think I only want you because I can't have you? Aren't you forgetting that I *have* had you? I told you then that I was looking for more than a casual fling with you. And that was before all this trouble." Josh was interrupted by a bunch of screaming kids who were playing tag around the parked cars as they were being washed. "We can't talk here. Have dinner with me. We've got to clear this up."

Pam agreed, and two hours later she was asking herself why. Josh was going to be picking her up in a few minutes for an early supper — someplace quiet, he'd said. She'd already changed her outfit three times before settling on the blue jersey dress she was now wearing. The skirt was flared and swirled around her legs as she restlessly paced across her living room. The sound of her matching blue high-heel shoes on the hardwood floor was grating on her nerves, so she stopped pacing and sat in her rocking chair.

Which was she more afraid of? That Josh was lying or that he was telling the truth when he said he loved her? Because if by loving her he meant that he wanted to possess her, then loving her wasn't enough. He'd warned her that he was going to woo and court her until she'd given in. Was telling her that he loved her just another step in the war of seduction he'd been waging against her? She didn't know, but she had to find out. *That's* why she'd agreed to go to dinner with Josh and talk. She felt a little better having established that fact.

He arrived five minutes early, which was fine with Pam. She was tired of waiting. Josh had traded in his running clothes for a suit that was tailored to fit him perfectly. His white shirt and understated tie made him appear light-years away from the man who'd stood sopping wet in the parking lot and told her he loved her.

"It's still me," he murmured with that uncanny ability to read her mind. He smiled at her. "You look different too. I like your dress. It shows off your great legs, although not as much as those cutoffs did."

"It sounds like you preferred the cutoffs."

"I like you in whatever you wear. I like you when you're wearing nothing at all. I like you period. Aside from loving you, that is."

Pam wondered how long she'd be able to hold out when he talked to her like that. No longer than a few seconds, that was for sure! But even if he was telling the truth about loving her, there was still the problem of what loving meant to Josh.

"Of course, you can be impossibly stubborn," Josh added as a teasing postscript.

"So can you," she retorted.

"See, yet another thing we have in

common. Are you ready to leave now?"

Pam nodded.

She was surprised to find that Josh was driving a very sedate-looking sedan in a non-descript beige.

"It's a rental," he explained as he held the passenger door open for her. "I haven't gotten around to buying one yet."

"What about the Ferrari?" she asked.

"I sold it before I relocated to Chicago. I didn't have the heart to put it through a winter up here."

"Come on, our winters aren't that bad."

"Not if you're a polar bear."

"Spoken like a true Californian."

Josh corrected her statement. "I went to college in California, but I grew up in Utah and Arizona. My dad and mom still live in Arizona."

"And your brothers and sisters?"

"Are spread all over the country."

"It must have been nice growing up with brothers and sisters." She sounded wistful. "Were you the oldest?"

"No, I'm right in the middle. My brother and one sister are older."

"How'd you get to be so bossy when you've got an older sister and brother?"

"How'd you get to be so bossy when you're an only child?" he countered.

"I'm not bossy!" she denied. "I'm not the one who orders other people around, you are. I'm the one who refuses to take orders. And you never answered my question."

"See what I mean?" he teased her. "Definitely bossy. And I imagine you got that way the same way I did."

"You and your vivid imagination," she said. "Go on, this should be interesting."

"If you're like me, then you prefer giving orders to receiving them because you've already received more than your fair share."

Josh was right on the mark, but it had never occurred to her that he might have similar reasons for acting the way he did.

When she made no reply, he said, "What, no caustic comments? No dramatic denials?"

"No."

"Does that mean I'm right?"

"Yes, but you don't have to gloat about it."

"As if I would do such a thing," he murmured. He took his eyes off the busy traffic long enough to give her a teasing look.

"You know you'd do such a thing, and you frequently have in the past."

"When have I ever gloated?" he demanded.

"When I got off that boat in Bermuda after getting stuck on board."

"It was a ship," he reminded her, "not a boat, and I wasn't gloating."

"No? What would you call this?" She mimicked his expression.

"I'd call it cute," he answered.

"It must have lost something in the translation," she muttered. "Where is this restaurant you're taking me to? I hope by 'someplace quiet and intimate' you didn't mean your place," she added as a sudden suspicion came to mind.

"The idea did cross my mind," he admitted. "But I decided against it. We'd never get any talking done."

"Pretty sure of yourself, aren't you," she retorted huffily.

"I have to be if I'm going to convince you that I love you."

Once again Pam didn't know what to say, so she remained quiet until they arrived at the restaurant. Inside, small booths were separated by partitions of stained glass and hanging plants, making it an ideal place to hold a private conversation.

"The filet mignon is very good here," Josh told her. "But the choice is yours."

To his surprise, she selected the filet, but her mind was clearly not on food.

After their waiter had taken their order, Josh made a suggestion. "Look, would you feel better if we put our personal discussion on hold until after the meal?"

"Yes." Pam welcomed the delay and stuck to neutral subjects over dinner, but when their after-dinner coffee was served, she knew her time was running out. "Do you want cream?" she asked, trying to stall a bit longer.

"I want *you*," he answered in a husky voice. "And I want to talk to you about it." He removed the tiny cream pitcher from her grasp and took her hand in both of his. "I think it's time we got a few things straight." He paused, waiting for her to meet his gaze before continuing. "First off, I meant what I said. I do love you. I didn't mean to blurt it out like that; I know the circumstances were hardly romantic. And I know that you're hesitant to trust me again, which is why I want to be honest with you and lay all my cards on the table. Are you willing to do the same?"

She nodded warily.

"Okay. Then tell me what you're afraid of."

"What makes you think I'm afraid?" she countered.

"This is the time for honesty, remember." He gave her hand a disapproving tug. "No more defenses. Are you afraid I'm going to lie to you again, hurt you in some way, what?"

"I'm afraid of a lot of things. That you think you know what's best for me, that you think you can control me, that you'd use my feelings to make me dependent on you." Once she'd started, the words just came tumbling out. "The first time I met you I knew you were a man used to being in charge. I'm not going to allow anyone to take charge of me again."

"Because of your father?"

"He was my adoptive father and yes, I feel that way because of him. Because of what he did to me."

"Tell me about it."

She looked away. "I don't like talking about it. There's no use crying over spilled milk."

Josh shook his head at her stoic resistance. "Spilled milk has got to be cleaned up or it gets sour. Talk to me."

She was quiet for so long that Josh thought she was going to ignore his plea. Then she finally began to speak in a voice so flat he almost didn't recognize it as being hers. "My parents died in a car accident when I was seven. Because there were no other close relatives, I was placed in a state children's home for a year until I could be placed permanently with a foster or an adoptive family. I was adopted by the Warners when I was eight."

When she stopped talking, Josh caressed her hand reassuringly. "Go on."

"My new father was a vice-principal at a high school on the south side of Chicago. They put him in charge of discipline because he was so good at it. Mr. Freeze, the kids used to call him, and they were right. He wasn't capable of any kind of real emotion. The only thing he was capable of was controlling those around him. He completely intimidated my adoptive mother. His authority wasn't to be questioned."

She had to stop again and swallow. Her throat felt dry and constricted. Wanting to get the rest of the story over with, she continued in a fast, tense voice. "He said that everything he did was for my own good, that he knew what was best for me. When he took me into his house he put me under his thumb. I left as soon as I was eighteen. I haven't had any contact with them since then. I later heard through a friend that they'd disowned me."

"Your adoptive father sounds like a real s.o.b." His voice was rough, and his eyes reflected his distress. "You really believe that I'm like him?"

"I'm not sure."

He looked as if her words had mortally wounded him. "You think I'm incapable of feeling any kind of real emotion?"

She felt his pain as if it were her own and she regretted her thoughtless words. "No, I didn't mean that you're like him in that way. Not at all."

"In what way, then?"

212

"I told you — you're the kind of man who's used to being in control, the kind who's used to giving orders."

"Okay, I can understand why you feel the way you do about taking orders. But have I really tried to take charge of you that much? If I have, I certainly haven't succeeded," he noted wryly. "I don't want to control you. You rarely do what I tell you to. You definitely have a mind of your own and that's what made me fall in love with you. You do what you feel you have to despite what I have to say about it. You're a strong woman, Pam. Strong enough to handle a strong man."

The idea of handling Josh was provocatively appealing, but Pam was still unconvinced.

He was getting frustrated. "What do I have to say to get through to you?"

"What do you want from me?" she asked with asperity.

"I want to share my life with you. I want you to share your life with me." His voice grew louder with every sentence. "I want you to love me. I want to know if you want the same things I do."

"I don't know. I need more time to get used to this."

Josh gave her a brooding look. She saw the turbulent emotions in his eyes before a

213

shutter came down. She got the uneasy impression that he'd just reached some sort of decision.

"You said you want to share your life with me," she reminded him. "For me, that includes sharing your thoughts. Don't shut me out when you get upset."

"You said you needed more time. You've got it. I'm leaving for a two-week business trip the day after tomorrow," he told her. "While I'm gone I want you to think about what I've said and remember what we shared in Bermuda. Will you do that?"

She nodded. Two weeks! She wouldn't see him for two whole weeks? During the drive back to her apartment Pam tried to come to terms with her emotions. She missed Josh already. She didn't want him to leave, but she wasn't capable of saying the words to make him stay. Not yet.

After accompanying Pam to her front door, Josh pulled a folded sheet of paper from his inner jacket pocket and handed it to her.

"What's this?" she asked.

"The date and time of my return flight. If you decide you want to share your life with me, then meet my plane. If you don't come, I'll know you're really not interested and I won't bother you again." The look he gave her was direct and incredibly complicated.

"Think about it, Pam." He brushed his thumb over her lips before turning and walking away from her.

Pam just stood there. She couldn't believe that he was actually leaving without even kissing her good-bye! Tears welled up and threatened to spill onto her cheeks. She had to get inside her apartment before she really started crying.

She'd just opened the door and was about to step inside when she felt a hand on her shoulder. Startled, she looked over her shoulder to see Josh.

He didn't say a word. He simply pulled her into his arms and kissed her with unrestrained hunger. She responded with equal passion, knowing he was kissing her good-bye again.

Pam's heart ached. She didn't want to think about all the things dividing them, about all the problems. There would be time enough for that when he was gone. For now she just wanted to hold him as he was holding her — tightly, fiercely, desperately.

His mouth slanted across hers, consuming her with a need so forceful it was almost frightening. Then the fierce kiss was suddenly over as abruptly as it had begun.

"I love you." There was a note of despair in his rough voice. "Remember that." And then he left.

Even though Pam spent a lot of time thinking over the next few days, she couldn't seem to clarify her thoughts. So she took one afternoon off and spent it down at the beach. It was the same beach where Chuck Warner had dropped her into Lake Michigan when she'd been a frightened eight-year-old. As she sat there, she found herself comparing that mental image with one set on another beach, this time in Bermuda. That overexuberant college student had dumped her in the water, and Josh had come to her rescue immediately.

Suddenly it hit her. Why hadn't she seen it earlier? Josh wasn't like her adoptive father in any of the ways that really counted. Sure, on the surface the two were both strong and authoritative. But when confronted with a similar situation, even though it had been years apart, the two men had reacted very differently. Her father had used his strength in a manipulative way; Josh had used it in a caring way.

Once she took away that looming fear that Josh would control her as her father had, she was able to view her feelings for him very clearly. She loved Josh, and she believed him when he said he loved her. He was right. She was strong enough to handle a strong man — providing that man was Josh. She refused to let her past haunt her any longer. She buried it there on that beach, where it had first taken root.

Feeling like the weight of the world had just been lifted from her shoulders, Pam eagerly awaited Josh's return, and her new attitude was noticed by both Anita and Roger.

"Isn't Josh due back soon?" Anita asked, as she had every day since the flowers had stopped coming.

"Tomorrow at five twenty-five," Pam replied.

"Five twenty-five, huh? Does that mean you're going to be waiting for him when he gets in?"

"It certainly does." Her face was positively glowing.

"I'm glad, Pam. I hope it works out for you."

By late the next afternoon Pam wondered if anything would ever work out for her again. Fate had been against her all day. She'd had a terrible time at work. Her arm and shoulder were both stiff from the long hours she'd spent on the phone: first getting permission for a federal employee to carry his gun on board a flight from Chicago to Florida, then fighting with one of the airlines over an incorrect fare quote, then rebooking a set of reservations because a client had given her the wrong dates.

With that kind of track record, it shouldn't have surprised her to be stuck in a rush-hour traffic jam that turned the Kennedy Expressway into a three-mile-long parking lot. She broke half a dozen rules of the road in her desperate bid to get to the airport on time.

She checked her watch every two minutes. Five-fifteen. Five-seventeen. Five-nineteen. She was going to be late, she knew it! Why wasn't this lane moving? Why was everyone trying to turn into the arrivals lane? She hit the palm of her hand on the horn and yelled out her window. "Come on, move it up there!"

What if Josh arrived and she missed him? What if he thought she didn't love him, didn't want to be with him? What if she passed that cab ahead of her and left her car in that empty space up there along the curb? So what if that was the departures section. So what if she was two terminals away from his arrival terminal. She could run, couldn't she? She'd have to.

She zoomed ahead with the skill of a race car driver and confiscated the parking space ahead of two other cars that were waiting for it. She ignored the rantings of the other drivers as she rammed the gearshift into Park, and jumped out of the car. She didn't even stop to lock it.

At least she was wearing sandals, which made running uncomfortable but not impossible. She finally made it to the proper terminal at five forty-one. Panting breathlessly, she shoved her hair out of her eyes and anxiously scanned the display screen listing incoming flight times and arrival gates. Maybe his flight had been delayed. No sooner had that hope been formed than it was dashed. *Arrived on time*, the screen stated. Damn!

Now what should she do? Baggage, check the baggage claim area. If there was any justice in the world, Josh wouldn't have picked up his baggage yet. *What if he didn't check his luggage?* she asked herself as she raced down the escalator. *What if he only had carry-on luggage?*

Wait, wasn't that him over there, leaning down to pick up a suitcase?

"Josh!" She ran up to him and was ready to throw her arms around him, only to see when the man turned that he was a stranger.

Her heart dropped. She felt like collapsing on the floor and crying.

Someone tapped her on the shoulder. "Were you looking for me?"

She was almost afraid to look. No, her ears

hadn't deceived her. It was Josh! "You're still here!"

"Still waiting for you," he murmured as she threw herself into his outstretched arms. They closed around her with a strength that made her feel like she'd finally come home. This was where she belonged.

She clung to him as if he were her one hope left in life. They didn't even break apart to kiss, so strong was their need just to hold each other.

"I was so afraid you'd already left," she murmured against his shoulder. "I ran all the way here; I left my car back at terminal one. This isn't the way I planned it at all. I was supposed to be waiting for you at the gate, looking all sultry and sexy in this jumpsuit. I bought it just for you. But there's a horrendous traffic jam out there and everything got messed up. I'm so sorry I'm late." She knew her explanation was disjointed but she didn't care, because she knew Josh would be able to understand her.

"I was afraid you weren't coming," he admitted.

His words gave her the strength to lean away from him so that she could see his face. He was looking at her in that special way she now knew meant that he loved her. She cupped his cheek with her trembling hand.

Josh kissed her softly, tenderly, as if fearing that she might disappear. The intensity of her response convinced him that she wasn't going anywhere without him. The need for more privacy sent them hurriedly searching for her car.

"The car's right over there," she said.

And so it was. But not for long. The tow truck it was attached to pulled into traffic, and her Mustang was hauled along with it.

"Hey, wait a minute!" Pam exclaimed. "Where are you going with my car? Bring that back here! You can't do that!"

"Was that your car, lady?" a Chicago cop standing nearby asked her.

"Yes."

"It was parked in a no-parking zone." He handed her a ticket.

Josh plucked the ticket from her hands. "I'll take care of that. It's my fault you got it." He paused for a moment, waiting for her to dispute his claim. "What, no arguments?"

She shook her head. "I did a lot of thinking while you were gone. And I discovered that I don't mind being rescued by you. In fact, I kind of like it."

"Only kind of?"

"Okay, I'll confess: I could learn to love it." She took a deep breath before adding, "I already love you."

Josh's suitcase dropped onto the pavement as he grabbed her in his arms and twirled her around. "You love me?"

"I love you. And I can't wait to show you how much."

"You don't have to wait," he decided with a wicked grin. As soon as he set her feet back onto the sidewalk, he took her by the hand and led her right across the street — straight to the registration desk of the conveniently located O'Hare Hilton.

Ten minutes later they were in their own room on the sixth floor, with a Do Not Disturb sign on the door.

"Alone at last!" Pam declared with a dramatic sigh.

That sigh turned into a moan as Josh stole the smile from her lips. His kiss was slow and warm, telling her that they had all the time in the world. His mouth moved sensuously over hers, and she melted against him.

She hadn't paid much attention to what he was wearing, but now her main concern was to seductively remove all the barriers between them, starting with *his* clothes first. She slid his jacket from his broad shoulders, then undid his tie. Now Josh was the one who smiled as his kisses strayed from the creamy smoothness of her lips to the equally smooth curve of her cheek. While she unbuttoned his shirt, he smoothed aside her hair so that he could kiss the vulnerable side of her neck.

Pam shivered and tilted her head, giving him better access to the line of her throat. Her movement meant that she could no longer see what she was doing, forcing her to rely on her sense of touch as she finished unfastening his shirt before peeling it away from his warm skin. Now she was free to caress him, and she did, with both her teasing fingers and adoring mouth.

Moaning deep in his throat, Josh thrust his hands through her dark hair and guided her mouth back to his. This time he shared a series of kisses with her, each one becoming increasingly intimate. Suddenly she felt the room tilt alarmingly as Josh scooped her into his arms and carried her to the bed.

"You seem to have this insatiable desire to sweep me off my feet," Pam noted with approval.

"Where you're concerned, I've got an insatiable desire, period," he muttered. He let her pull back the bedspread and blankets before setting her down on the king-size bed.

She tugged him down after her and explored his bare back with restless hands. How had she managed so long without him? Would he still shiver if she ran her nails along the small of his back? She was delighted to discover that he did.

Josh was delighted to discover that her jumpsuit possessed large, easy-to-undo buttons, which made it easy for him to remove it. Soon her jumpsuit and his trousers joined the tumbled bedspread on the floor at the foot of the bed. Seconds later her lacy bra was added to the pile.

Josh drew in a shaky breath as he gazed down at her with hungry eyes. "It's been so long."

"Too long," she murmured.

"I've missed you so much." His hand trembled slightly as he reached out to touch her. He cupped one breast in the palm of his hand, while his mouth hovered over the creamy slope of the other.

"Do you like this?" he whispered so close to her silky skin that she could feel every word.

She shivered and moaned when he stroked her with the tip of his tongue.

"Does that mean you like it?" he asked in a tenderly sexy voice.

"Yes . . . Josh . . . please, don't stop."

He didn't stop until she was writhing with pleasure. Only then did he pause to remove his underwear and hers. Now it was her turn to return some of the ecstasy he'd given her. She caressed him with sultry passion, doing wicked things to him. Josh's ragged gasp warned of his waning control.

Her smile was seductive. "Does that mean you like it?"

"Let me show you how much I like it," he murmured. His hands swirled over her with devilish skill as he tantalized her inner warmth.

They were both out of control when he finally came to her. With a cry of unbearable excitement, Pam eagerly received him. He fulfilled their mutual need with slow, heated strokes and impelling thrusts that heightened her pleasure, and his own. His movements sent her spinning into a world of sensual delight as her entire body contracted and then burst in ecstasy. Feeling the moment he'd been waiting for, Josh joined her, shuddering in release.

Cradling her in his arms, he rolled with her until they lay side by side. "I love you," he murmured.

"I love you, too," she whispered. "So much."

"Pam, I want to marry you." He braced himself as if preparing for her argument.

She didn't make any. "Oh, good."

"Good?"

She nodded. "I put in a tentative request to reserve the chapel at St. Michael's church for the ceremony."

"Oh, you did, did you?"

"It was only a tentative booking," she added uncertainly. "It still has to be confirmed. But that is where you first told me you loved me. Outside in the parking lot, remember. What do you think of the idea?"

"I think that you've been a handful of trouble since the first second I laid eyes on you."

"Is that a complaint?" she demanded.

"No, it's a compliment." He held her breasts in the palms of his hands. "You know how I love having my hands full!"

The employees of Thorndike Press hope you have enjoyed this Large Print book. All our Large Print titles are designed for easy reading, and all our books are made to last. Other Thorndike Press Large Print books are available at your library, through selected bookstores, or directly from the publishers.

For more information about titles, please call:

(800) 257-5157

To share your comments, please write:

Publisher
Thorndike Press
P.O. Box 159
Thorndike, Maine 04986

LF Linz LARGE PRINT
Linz, Cathie
A handful of trouble

$26.00